ABOUT THE AUTHOR

Jennifer Manson is a writer and business woman. Born in New Zealand, she now lives in the United Kingdom. She is the author of six novels, including *The Moment of Change*, *Tasha Stuart interviews...*, *The Old Occidental Writers' Hotel*, *Law of Attraction* and *Inventor*, and two life philosophy books, *Easy – Stories from an effortlessly created life* and *Truth*.

Inventor

Jennifer Manson

First published in New Zealand in 2011

ISBN 978-0-473-18529-9

Cover design by Jay Ganda, Red Dot Design

www.jennifermanson.co.nz

ACKNOWLEDGEMENTS

To my writing buddy, poet Kerrin P. Sharpe;

To my reader, Vicki Slade, and my editor, Tanya Tremewan;

To David Clarkson, Ralph Brown and Dr Rodney Ford, for your fantastic support;

To the design team of the Porsche Boxster, genii and artists;

To Alex, Jono and Paul;

Thank you.

All characters in this book are fictitious
and any resemblance to real persons,
living or dead, is purely coincidental.

This book is set in Christchurch, New Zealand,
before the earthquakes of 2010 and 2011.
Sadly, some locations are not now as they were.

1

In the deep of midwinter in a beach-front campground in Canterbury, New Zealand, a young, small woman emerged from a custom-made, down-filled hammock. She folded back the flap of her frost-covered tent and blinked in the morning light. Her nose wrinkled against the cold and she experimented with a wide exhale which condensed and floated, beginning a slow, chaotic shift away from her. She went back into the tent for her shoes, then picked her way cautiously towards the shower block. From there she progressed to the kitchen where she had left a box of supplies. She returned to the tent with her morning lifeline, a cup of hot, black coffee. Time to start the day.

Everything in the tent was made to precise specifications, refined and reduced so that within half an hour of any given moment she could have it packed up into one medium-sized box in her car ready to move on to the next location, the next chapter of her life.

She kept coming back here, however. In the orbit of her life this was one fixed point among a very few. The attractions were the sound of the sea, the loneliness of the end of the road and the relatively easy proximity, only twenty minutes' drive, to her brother's house in the city. There she had an unfailingly warm welcome, lovingly fraternal concern and a well-equipped workshop for whatever was the latest project.

The small metal table on which she placed her coffee was the only solid surface in her home; everything else was crafted from telescoping carbon fibre poles and high-tech modern fabric so that it would shrink and roll into the smallest of spaces. A table needs to be flat. Everything else can flex and bend and still do its job. The chair, a variation on the standard director's design, moulded itself to her shape and she leaned back, sipping her coffee and thinking.

In a month, spring would be here, and the outdoor market circuit would begin again. Just as well: with the new designs she was working on, money was running low. She was losing weight, she knew, but when it came to a choice between materials and food, there was no question. Bob would feed her, and anyway, she often forgot to eat when she was absorbed, even if a meal was waiting steaming at her elbow as she worked.

Jackie zipped the tent and backed her car out into the roadway. There was no-one else here at this time of year, and mid-week. Even the permanent caravans were empty. Sometimes the campground owners were around when she checked in, sometimes not. If they saw her tent they knew she'd be in some time soon with payment. They did her a really good deal, less than half the normal daily rate, because of how much time she spent here. Another reason to return, so they reasoned, and they were right.

Bob would be out at work but she knew the combination to his workshop. Just stop in at the house for a moment to say hi to her sister-in-law, smile at the baby and ruffle the hair of her nephews. In a year or two she'd let the boys join her in the workshop, see what she was doing, but not yet. They were still too young to be safe around the tools and materials. Especially if she was welding, like today.

Sandra looked frazzled but she greeted Jackie warmly. She and Bob were good people. Such good people. When Jackie remembered this it gave her a glow of warmth – when she wasn't so totally focused on the current project that she hardly knew who she was, let alone anyone else. Like today.

INVENTOR

2

At five-thirty, her brother drove up and parked outside the workshop. Jackie didn't hear his car, or the sound of the door closing. Half an hour later one of the young boys appeared. "Mum says do you want dinner?"

Jackie looked up from her work and blinked. After a beat of a few seconds she looked at her watch. A few more seconds passed, and she put down her tools. "Hey, Seymour. Thanks. Tell her I'll be in in a minute."

The child disappeared. Jackie eased her back, slowly arching upwards with audible clicks and creaks. Nine hours. Where had they gone?

The kitchen was warm and bright. Her brother grinned as she stepped into the room. "New project?"

"How could you tell?"

"You look more human when you've just been building stock."

"You telling me I don't look human?"

"Not nearly. You've got that alien expression, wide, wild eyes. And your hair! What do you do, twist machine oil into it while you're working."

Jackie put her hand up to her head. It was possible. Her hands were black and greasy, and she sometimes ran them through her hair when she was thinking. "I'll go wash up."

In the bathroom she glanced into the mirror. There were black streaks on her forehead and right cheek, and her hair was indeed standing up strangely. She swallowed, took a moment to think, then leaned out of the bathroom door.

"Sandra? Do I have time for a shower?"

"Sure. Dinner'll be on the table in ten."

Bob appeared in the hall with a clean sweatshirt. "No point putting that old stuff back on. I'm just putting Clara to bed. See you in a bit."

The water took a couple of minutes to run hot. Jackie found a clean towel in the cupboard under the sink and took the kids' shampoo from the end of the bath. Five minutes under the water brought her back into her body from the limbo space she occupied when she was fixed on a new idea. She towel-dried her hair, slipping back into plans and designs, and wandered out into the family room, clean, fresh and once again preoccupied.

The conversation washed over her, the boys talking about their day, telling their dad every detail. Jackie flowed in the tide of it without consciously listening, her face reflecting pleasure and surprise at the appropriate moments, but without really hearing the words.

"So what is it this time, Sis? Something big?"

Again the delay of a few telling seconds before her reply. "Sort of. Not really. More of a refinement – for the fabric furniture. The rolling concept's good, but it's still a little slow. I'm working on a concertina idea, like a roman blind, so when it's time to pack up I just pull on a couple of strings, wrap a Velcro tie around and voila! The tricky bit's where to put the string. Too far out and you need three hands to do it; too far in, or only one string and you don't get a neat fold." She was sliding out of the present again, back to the workshop and her day's slow experimental progress. Sandra, Bob and Seymour watched her. Augustus, three years old, was sculpting his mashed potato, oblivious.

Sandra's face wrinkled. "So it's still about packing up and moving on. Don't you want to have a house some day? Security? I hate to think of you alone in that tent. What if somebody broke in?"

Jackie looked at her sister-in-law with sympathy, put her hand out onto hers to reassure her, as if she were the one needing comfort. "It's okay, really."

"But don't you want ..."

Jackie continued to gaze into her sister-in-law's face. "You know, it's interesting, that you ask me that. I've been thinking about it a lot recently, the ways people try to help each other."

"What about it?" Sandra asked. Bob looked from one to the other, his body suddenly tense.

"People often try to help other people get what they themselves would want. You and Bob have this great life: home, family, everything you want. And it's normal to think other people would want that, too. But what if they don't?"

"Who wouldn't want a home and a family?"

Bob reached out a hand as if to intervene, but the movement stopped halfway, suspended. Jackie continued speaking. "That's just it. Who? But maybe there are people. I like moving around. I like travelling light. And when I look at people who society would say were underprivileged, I wonder how much of it is that they don't have what they want, and how much of it is that they are more like me, that they don't have the same priorities. Maybe permanence is not a priority. Maybe possessions are not a priority. Maybe that transient existence is actually what they want, moving from relationship to relationship, home to home. And maybe part of the reason it doesn't work out is that our society isn't set up to tolerate it very well."

Sandra frowned. "That doesn't make sense to me."

"Well, it's only a theory. I'll have to ask around to see if it actually applies. In the meantime, I'm working on better ways to make the nomad's existence work. For me if not for anybody else. And the problem of the hour is, how to make the concertina concept work in practice."

Bob breathed out, relaxing now the conversation was back to the practical. "I'll take a look after dinner. Maybe I can help."

"I still don't understand it. But I'm not as clever as the two of you." Sandra picked up two plates from the table, moving towards the sink as if this fact were a matter of pride for her. Bob and Jackie grinned at each other.

"You're amazing. Thanks for dinner, it was delicious."

Bob bent over the vice, experimentally tugging on the string mechanism Jackie had set up. "I didn't want to ask in front of Sandra, but exactly where are you planning to conduct this questioning?"

"About whether the transient life is choice or default?"

"That's it."

"Well, I need to ask the so-called underprivileged."

"And that would be where?"

"I don't know ... maybe a mall?"

Bob closed his eyes and rubbed a hand over his face. "Just be careful, Sis. That lifestyle often comes with a large degree of chaos. Drugs. Alcohol. Crime."

"You worry too much."

"Just promise me you won't approach anybody who's actually high."

"All right."

"Or anyone with a pit bull, rottweiler, anything like that."

"You know, you judge people, you don't give them a chance."

Bob looked at his sister, twenty-one years old, five foot two, thin to the bone, damp hair fluffing around her heart shaped face, his old grey sweatshirt hanging to her knees. "Please, Jackie. Just promise me."

"I lead a charmed life. I'll be okay."

He turned away from her to hide the fear on his face.

"Okay. If it will make you happy, I'll be careful."

"Thanks."

Jackie crawled into her hammock, pulling the luxurious built-in down cover over herself, wriggling down happily. A day inventing. A good day.

3

It was late September, the first of the summer markets. Jackie wandered around watching her fellow stallholders setting up. It took them so long. Her stall was up in three minutes flat, and her entire stock held in two small, light boxes. People made things so much harder than they needed to be.

There were a few new faces. The market world is like a beach full of driftwood: new pieces washing up all the time, and just as often washing away again. The old-timers, further up the beach, were longer-term fixtures, but sometimes one of them would go. Jackie trawled through her mind to think who was not here. The layout this year was a little different, and she hated the idea it might be weeks before she noticed an old friend was missing. Then there would be the inevitable asking around to see if anyone knew what had happened. This was the only part of the transient life she didn't enjoy, the thought that people could disappear forever and she wouldn't even know they had needed help.

It was great catching up with people, however, even if only briefly. There would be more time to talk at the end of the day, maybe go for a drink, catch up on the winter's news.

"Here, let me hold that." She reached out to pull on a piece of canvas, hold it taut while an old metal fitting was forced into place. "You need one of my lightweight stalls. I've made some new adjustments."

"You say that every year. This old friend does me fine."

Jackie looked over at the dented van full of heavy wooden furniture. "I don't know how you do it, Frampton. That stuff weighs a ton."

"I like it. It keeps me grounded." He looked Jackie up and down. "I wouldn't want to think that at any time I might just blow away."

"I like blowing where the wind takes me. You should try it sometime."

He shook his head. "No. I like my routine. You know me."

Jackie grinned. "Yeah. Coffee later?"

"You got your little machine?"

"Yup."

"Then I'll be there."

Jackie returned to her stall and arranged her standard stock of chairs and early season tent stalls like her own for the other sellers ready to make the change. The table she sold from had been the box containing these items, the sides hinged with turning flat supports which either held the box shape or supported the various flaps that made up the table. Carbon fibre legs telescoped out on the same crossing system as the chair supports.

Under the table was a second container, a new experiment, Jackie's complete Life-in-a-Box. As a single item purchase it was expensive – selling one would keep her fed for six months – but as a fully furnished home for one or two people, it was the bargain of the century. She had hopes it might be one of the market regulars who bought the first one. Jackie knew that some of the stall holders were little more than hobbyists, making a small income from doing something they loved. Others, however, were shrewd business people, pulling in a six-figure income with the added joy of being self-employed and independent. It was some of these Jackie thought might be interested, ready to let go of the tyranny of solid walls and buy her tent, chairs, storage units, hammocks, all in the converted table/box, and take to the nomadic life like her. She'd moved away from her usual unobtrusive natural green for this experiment, making the tent in a multi-coloured carnival theme. It needed to attract attention, get people talking. There was no room for invisibility here.

Jackie adjusted her marketing images on the table and waited for the first customers to arrive.

By midday Jackie had made more than a fortnight's income, having sold three chairs and a couple of roll-up pictures. That was good. She needed more cash for new projects, materials. Experimenting could get expensive.

"I like this colour. Much better than that drab old green you keep bringing out year after year."

Jackie looked at Mike's peacock outfit, and at the colourful balls he was juggling. "I like to blend in."

"That was obvious. Why the change?"

Jackie laughed. "Thought it was time to get noticed. I should have done it years ago, I'm selling twice as much as usual."

"I'm not surprised. Tell me about this." He pointed to the images of the Life-in-a-Box.

"It's a copy of what I live in, but done up bright. Like the chairs, but a whole living set-up: beds, table, everything."

"And it all fits in this box?"

"The table is the box, but basically yes."

"Wow." The balls fell one, two, three into his hand. "Wow. And you made this?"

"Years ago. But I never thought of selling it till now."

Mike shook his head. "How did you survive! How did you not see this?"

"That's just it. I was surviving too well. I didn't think of it because I didn't need to. But now I need to up my income. I'm searching for my Holy Grail and I need to finance the quest."

"And what's your Holy Grail?"

"Something I've dreamed about since I was six and never had the guts to go after ..."

"Well?"

"You'll laugh."

"So? You believe in it, tell me."

A beat of hesitation. "Okay ... it's the ultimate invention, so simple, so fundamental, that it alters our very existence. So obvious that it instantly becomes part of every day. And it changes life for the better, for everyone, forever."

Mike's eyes widened. "What is it?" he whispered.

Jackie stared at him. "If I knew that, would I still be searching? Of course I don't know what it is, yet. But I know it's there. And I know I'll find it."

Mike leaned back in the red and orange chair and laughed. "You really had me going. Well, I'll buy this." He patted the arms. "Then I can say I was instrumental in this world change you're talking about, when it finally comes."

"You doubt me? You're laughing?"

"I do not doubt you. Not at all. But I am laughing. I'm always laughing. That's what you love about me. No, forget that – I won't take the chair, I'll take the whole box."

"The Life-in-a-Box? Really?"

"Really. I've been thinking it's time I moved on."

"Sarah?"

Mike grimaced. "It's been fading." He shrugged. "Time to draw a line."

"But that's terrible! I feel terrible! I don't want to do that to her."

"Don't worry. You didn't. She can blame it all on me. She would anyway. I can take this box, create a new life. By tonight I'll be gone."

Jackie hovered nervously, stalled halfway to picking up the box. "You can't. Really you can't. Not just because of me."

"I told you! It's not just because of you. Now, do you take credit cards?"

"You know I do."

"Well then. Let's do it."

4

Jackie leaned back as Mike sauntered away, the box tucked under his arm. She braced herself for a visit from Sarah, but when she passed an hour or so later she was humming lightly, vague and cheerful. He hadn't told her yet. Jackie's jaw jutted forward, lower teeth biting upper lip. Her eyes shifted sideways, avoiding Sarah's gaze. She reached under the table as if she were tidying stock, but Mike had bought half what she'd brought with her. There was nothing to do.

It was a good day. Early in the season she always did good trade with the other stall holders who were setting themselves up. As well as Mike's purchase she sold twelve chairs, three pictures and a market stand. Fantastic! As she closed up, her box almost empty, she was in the mood for celebrating. She leaned over into the next space, swallowing before she managed to produce a passably casual voice. "Hey, Zach. Fancy a drink? I'm buying."

"Show-off." Zach threw long, dark curls back off his forehead, his olive skin glowing with health.

"Don't complain. You know your time will come. Christmas market, that's your thing."

Zach continued wrapping a small clay angel. At his elbow was a box filled with tissue-wrapped items. "I should learn from you, make something robust."

"We all have to follow our path and passion. You'd be bored with something so practical."

"Still, one slip loading the van and I've lost a month's production."

"Pity me! I sold a month's production today. How am I going to keep up?"

"Shut up. Showing off again. Okay. You can buy me that drink. Or three, or four. Help me forget."

At the bar across the street, with the sounds of cool jazz sweeping the atmosphere smooth and Zach filling the pauses with observations on the clientele, Jackie faded out again, letting his words wash over her, chiming and contrasting with the various thoughts that flowed through her head. Occasionally an image or idea would pull her back and she would comment; mostly the sound was a lull for her, and she visibly relaxed as he talked on.

"You know, you're the weirdest audience ever."

She moved her eyes to his chin, then slowly up his face until she met his gaze. Her heart beat a little faster. "What do you mean?"

"I mean, I don't think you've heard a word I've said, and yet it's so peaceful talking to you, so calming. How do you do it?"

"I am listening. I like the sound of your voice."

Zach laughed. "Yeah. I can tell that. But what do you do with it?"

Jackie frowned, then twisted her face to the side. "What do you mean? I hear you. I relax. You're nice."

"You see, that's just it. For most people talking is a way of exchanging information. Tell me what I've been speaking about."

There was a long pause. "Well ..."

"Well?"

"I was seeing the place I go to up near Lake Coleridge. There's a hillside that slopes down and there's a green field in front of it. Then you look to the left and you see, in the distance, a higher mountain, bare of vegetation, with snow on the top most of the year. But with the perspective it looks smaller."

"And that relates to what I was saying, how?"

"The water in front is often glassy smooth – it's protected from the wind there – so you get this amazing reflection. Then further off the lake is choppier, a different mood."

"And again, how does this all fit?"

"You said about reflecting on life, the highs and the lows. And I thought of that. Horizontal symmetry. The flatness of water. Gravity. You said something about gravity. It was perfect – I had an idea for something I've been working on, how I can use gravity to make it work better."

"Reflecting on the highs and lows of life. You got that. And Gravity – it's a brand of coffee, by the way, I was talking about coffee. I can't figure out if I'm offended or amused or ..."

"You're not offended. You're charmed." Jackie blushed as she said it, and her hands tensed.

"And then you say something like that and I want to kiss you. But it would never work. I am charmed. You're right. But if I lived with you I think the charm might wear off in a very short time."

"And you see, that's something else I've been wondering about ..."

"What? Did you even hear what I said?"

"I sleep in a hammock, you see. Which is fine for one. But how would two people live together that way? Two people who wanted to sleep together. How would I fit a real bed into my box?"

"Jackie, it wasn't a proposition." Zach's expression was embarrassed, as if she'd caught him out, but she didn't notice.

"What wasn't?"

"That thing I said about you being charming. I said I couldn't live with you."

"I know that Zach. What are you talking about? Who was talking about us living together?" Her blush deepened.

Zach shook his head again, laughing and blushing too. "God! It's like talking to the Sphinx. Or some character from Alice in Wonderland."

"Well you keep asking me questions! I answer them. What did I do wrong?"

"It's okay, you didn't do anything wrong. You're right, it's charming."

She gazed at him, her expression relaxing. "You see, that's why I love being with you, I can be myself. Other people don't ..."

"Don't what?"

"Understand. It makes them uncomfortable."

Zach didn't answer, just looked at her, his eyes soft, an unconscious smile on his lips. He took a sip of his drink, then another, then drained his glass and held it up for a refill. Jackie watched him, nodding happily, until her attention was grabbed by another idea and her eyes slid out of focus once more.

5

The next day was a hammock day. They came upon Jackie occasionally. She knew it meant she had something to work out and she waited calmly, anticipating the revelation.

For a day or two it was fine. If the idea brewing took longer than that, it wasn't so easy drawing herself out of the depression the inactivity precipitated. As long as it was only a day. Or two.

On the third day, Tuesday, she began to be a little uneasy. Usually when this happened she at least knew the challenge she was likely to solve. This time she had no idea. Just the long-held assumption that in retrospect it would make sense. It always had before. Almost always.

She was just contemplating a foray to the kitchen, maybe a sandwich or two. Her mobile bleeped. This was getting more frequent. She didn't look at it. Whatever the messages had started out as, they would now be more and more urgent requests for a response. Bob. Or Zach. Wanting to know she was okay.

She sighed and rolled over, counterbalancing the swing of the hammock by pushing against the side with her foot. Perhaps it would be soon. Perhaps it would be the kind of idea that propelled her into immediate action, leaving behind this inert state like a moulting grasshopper's husk. She closed her eyes. Please, let it be that way. But she knew better than to expect it. Experience told her that after this long she would pay with a slow recovery.

Still, there were a few tricks she could try. Sometimes seeding an idea with random thoughts would get things going. Sometimes combing back through her thought processes for the last few days would reveal the direction of her unconscious.

What had there been? The first market of the season. Zach. Mike. Sarah. She grimaced when she thought of Sarah, alone now through the catalyst of Jackie's inventions. The painful thought made her reach for her phone, for distraction, whatever the communication might be.

Here, interesting. One from Mike. "Jackie! Call me!" She scrolled back to find the first of his. They were nearly all his. Here it was. Monday night. "Call me. Found someone for you to talk to."

She felt a small lift in her chest, the possibility of action. But not yet. Not yet. She put her thumb on the Reply button, then pulled it away again. She just wasn't up to it today. And she didn't know what would happen, didn't know if the plan she had brewing, whatever it was, would survive an interruption. She was superstitious about these small miracles of inspiration, followed a ritual, followed the rules that had developed over years of circumstantial association: she'd had this good idea in this place – go there again; she'd had this insight after a week of stillness – listen to that voice that told her to stop; she'd had this success while using this screwdriver – keep it safe, keep it special, certainly never, ever, let anyone borrow it. These flashes of brilliance she thought of as the essence of her soul. She might be nothing without them. Mike had an opportunity for her. She'd just have to hope it would keep.

On the Saturday, market day, $70 stall fee wasted, she sat up, stood up, her eyes bright and wide, and pulled a piece of paper onto the table. It had started. Just doodlings at first, a few scattered words which made no sense, alone, or with each other. Breakfast. Maybe that was just hunger. Orange.

Was that a fruit or a colour or an English phone company? Or hunger again? Blackfoot. What was blackfoot? She did a quick internet search and turned up a range of possibilities: a Native American tribe, New Zealand shellfish and a miniature two-wheel-drive monster truck. Which one was it? Was it all three? That would make a great combination, cultural and food tours, what about it?

The sketches were stranger, corkscrew shapes in decreasing circles, mansions like she used to draw when she was ten, seagulls and mountains and rivers and railway tracks. She wrote down 'transport,' 'haggle', 'spot'.

She had scattered the words around. Now she ran her eyes over them looking for links, experimenting with anagrams. Nothing. She tried again. Still nothing. The hope and expectation that had risen in her chest peaked and subsided. She turned over the paper and went back to bed.

Another day passed.

6

On Monday morning she heard a thumping outside her tent. Bleary-eyed she reached for her phone. Five o'clock. She noticed there were another twelve texts. She had turned the sound off last night when the bleeping pulled her out of her wretched dullness, a state she could almost call sleep. Each time it just brought home how bad she was feeling.

The thumping continued. She heard the sound of Velcro separating, deeply familiar. This was something she herself had designed. Someone was putting up one of her tents. A light came on and she saw a shadow cross her north wall. Her eyes moved back and forth, following her thoughts. The easiest way to find out would be to look.

Her feet hit the cold floor and she reached for socks. The shadow passed again. Now it was whistling. Her coat hung on a hook. For modesty's sake she pulled it over her nightgown. She blinked again. The space in her chest was constricting.

Nervous. I'm nervous. That's not right.

She took a deep breath and threw back her door flap.

"Mike. I thought it was you."

He was backlit; Jackie walked around him until, as he followed, the light shone on his face.

"Yeah. Look at me. I've been looking for you for ages, and here you are. You're not easy to track down. Cell phone broken?"

"I'm in a creative phase. You're interrupting." She wasn't trying to offend him, or make him go. Just stating a fact. "I may lose my idea if you stay."

"Think positive. I might give you the answer. Isn't that true? I just might."

Jackie bit her lip as she absorbed this idea. External circumstances had helped her process before. Mike was right. The random element often brought answers.

"Why are you here?"

"I got this Life-in-a-Box, but as they say in real estate, it's all about location. It's fit for a king if you find the right view. But if you just think about cheapness, you end up looking at the fence of a suburban hell. You've got the right idea here, though. This is fantastic."

Jackie turned towards the sound of the waves. Through the trees she could just see the white shine of the water as it rolled onto the beach, dotted lines of irregular breaking waves interrupted by the silhouettes of the pine trees.

"It's pretty good, yeah. Wait till you see it."

"I can feel it. You know me, it's all about feeling."

Jackie's nose twitched. She liked Mike, but she wasn't totally sure he was honest. She wasn't totally sure she was comfortable with him and no-one else nearby.

"I don't usually feel like this." She flinched as she said it. Sometimes the wrong part of her thoughts came out. The bits that should be spoken remained silent, and other bits, which might be better private, formed into words. She bit her lip. There was a sense of helplessness.

"Like what? Don't say you fancy me. I've just got rid of Sarah."

"That's what I mean. That wasn't nice, what you did to her."

"You know what I always say about relationships?"

Jackie didn't answer. Mike continued as if she had.

"That people know what they're getting into. They know who they're taking on. It makes me mad when they say they don't. 'He just turned on me'; 'I never thought she'd have an affair.' Well, actually, 'he' was a bastard from the start; 'she' was always a slut. People spend half their lives in denial and half in indignant surprise. And they cry to each other. Well don't cry to me."

Jackie nodded. She felt good to know her gut had been right. "So that's why I don't fancy you, Mike. I already know you're a bastard."

He tipped back his head and laughed. "I wasn't actually talking about me. But touché. You're not one of the naïve ones."

She tilted her head, a question. "Actually I think that's exactly what I am. And what you're advocating. But it's not interesting to me. I want to know what you're doing here."

He pulled his head back and gave himself a little shake. "Not interesting . . ? Boy ... Well, what am I doing here? Two things. One, I wanted a place for my palace, fit for my palace. And two, I know a guy who's interested in helping you with your inventions. He's in marketing."

"So when do I meet him?"

"It's not quite that simple. He's a shark. He'd eat you alive. You need someone to protect you. A business partner. Me."

Jackie turned away. “No.” She headed back to her tent.

“No! What do you mean ‘no’?”

“It’s a fairly simple word.” She hesitated, then turned again. He stepped close and she leaned back away from him.

“Why not?”

“Because I don’t trust you. And I trust myself.”

“But, Honey, what you’ve got is brilliant. You’re brilliant. You just need a little help to leverage it.”

“Listen, Mike. You’re charming. Good company. But I don’t trust you. I’d sooner sleep with you than get in bed with you in business.”

Again, Mike’s head jerked back. “Not a very ladylike way of putting it,” he said, finally.

“But that’s what it feels like, the way you ask it. Creepy. It makes me want to go take a shower.” She turned away again.

Mike took a step after her and grabbed her arm, turning her back. “You’re not very polite.”

She looked up at him, clear eyes glinting in the darkness. He let go, stepped back. “You don’t really care how polite I am. You just don’t like that I said no. That I see through you. Whatever you say about people in denial, it’s convenient for you.” She moved towards her tent. Her cheeks flexed quickly up towards her eyes, and her forehead creased for a brief moment. “I don’t think I feel very good about this. About this conversation. About you staying there.”

“You can’t make me leave. It’s a free country.” As he said it, he looked awkward. His eyes shifted nervously. He couldn’t admit now that he’d actually rather go.

Jackie stepped backwards, opening her tent. "But I would like to meet this guy. Without you. Can I? Can you tell me who he is?"

"Why would I do that?"

"What have you got to gain by not? And we're friends, aren't we?"

"Are we? After all you said?"

She shrugged. "Why not? I knew all of that before, and we were. It would be pretty sad for you if no-one who knew you would be friends with you."

Mike's mouth pulled forward and down. His eyes shifted to the left and stayed there, fixated on a point in the darkness.

"So can I?"

"Um ... it would be better if I introduced you."

"But you'd tell him we're not partners?"

"You ..."

"It's okay. I really can handle myself. No shark's getting me."

Mike nodded, stupidly.

"Thanks. Let me know when."

She pushed back the tent flap again and closed it behind her. She flicked on a light. She sat at her table, idly staring at the back of her doodle paper. The vaguest outline of the images and words showed through. The narrowing corkscrew intrigued her, and she forgot about Mike. The sound of his car door opening and closing, the roar of the engine, didn't penetrate to her conscious thoughts. An hour later, when it got light, she looked up in surprise, suddenly aware of the human emptiness. She stepped out again. His tent was half constructed. The box sat on the ground.

Jackie sighed. Her eyes drooped sadly. “Poor Mike,” she said, aloud, as she picked up the pieces and put together his world for when he came back.

7

Back in her tent she couldn't settle. The stillness of deep contemplation was gone. For a while she sat at the table, sketching, staring into space, but she needed movement. She picked up her toilet bag and headed for the shower.

Walking back she felt the real world in focus. She was annoyed, and tried to calm herself. "Trust the process. It always works out." When she'd described this to Zach, this way of living and working, he'd asked how she could stand it.

"Zach." She closed her eyes and brought his kind face into her mind, almost like the real thing in front of her. Maybe he was free.

She sent him a text, but didn't wait for him to answer. Whether she could see him or not, she needed to head back into town. She was too restless here.

There had been no answering bleep by the time she passed the turnoff to her brother's factory on the north edge of town. The steering wheel turned of its own accord and she found herself pulling into his car park, waving through the window where he was sitting at his computer. Bob made children's play equipment, their father's design, so popular that he just produced the same item again and again and again. She didn't know how he stood it.

"Hey, Sis."

"Hey there. Are you busy?"

"Just trying to get these accounts out. Anything up?"

"No. Just bored, really. I don't want to get in your way."

Bob peered at her. "They can wait. Talk."

"Well. There's something brewing. But I can't get at it."

"But you're okay?"

"Yes." She picked up a picture of the play frame, standard tubing in the shape of a house, four legs up to a waist-height bar on both sides, sloping poles running up to a ladder-like structure along the ridge. "Why don't you at least let me design a tent to go over this? Kids would love it. We could do it like castle walls, or a cottage. You could go back to everyone who's ever bought from you, sell to them again. You know one-off customers are never going to make you rich. You have to sell to them fresh every time. You'll wear yourself out."

"I don't need to be rich. Surviving would be nice. But not rich."

"Well, survive then. Is it that bad?"

"You know me. I hate accounts. They make me grumpy."

"Really, Bob. We don't need the high-tech fabric that I use, something halfway. We'd make a prototype, take some photos, email out and get pre-sales. That would pay to make them. No risk."

"I don't have their email addresses."

"Bob! What do you have? Phone numbers?"

He shook his head.

"Names and addresses?"

"Yep. Got those."

"Good grief. You're in the dark ages. But we can start from there, see what numbers we can get, start putting together an email list. Get me the file."

"Now? But we were in the middle of a conversation!"

"Were we?"

"You were going to tell me what's been happening with you."

"Nah. It's boring. I'll do this. I'll think at the same time."

Bob hesitated, then turned to an old grey filing cabinet. "You'll have to go through them. They're filed by date."

Jackie took the folder out of his hand. "What's this, Bob? There are bills, memos, your statements, all mixed in together."

"I told you. They're filed by date. That's January this year. The rest of the months are here, and here, and here."

"But how do you go back to anything? What does your accountant do? What if you want to look something up? How do you know where to find it?"

Bob's mouth worked and he looked at the floor. "I can usually remember, approximately. I look through."

"Wow."

"What? Shut up. I was doing fine before you walked in here criticising."

"I'm not criticising, I just ... look, let me past." She reached for the filing cabinet. "How far back does it go?"

"Eight years." He walked across the room and pulled out the bottom drawer of another cabinet. "July," he said, proudly. "It was my birthday. It all starts here." He reached out to hand the file to Jackie, but then pulled it back, fondly removing a yellow, dog-eared scrap of paper. "My first customer. That was before I got the receipt pad. But here it is. Mrs Carstairs. 49 Rugby St. I wonder if she's still there. The kids would have grown out of it long ago."

"While you reminisce, I'll get going. I don't need that one yet. I'll work backwards."

"Why?"

"Because they'll be there, and they'll still be using them. No point phoning the ones who won't."

Bob nodded. He stretched his shoulders back. "I think that idea must be near coming."

"What makes you say that?"

"You're clear. Logical. That only happens when you're getting an idea."

"No it doesn't. Usually I'm hopeless ..." She stopped speaking. She tried never to let anyone see her in that state. Not surprising Bob didn't know it. He was talking about the state he did see, the one that came after the idea.

"Well, sometimes you're like this. Let's hope it's a good one."

"Why?"

"It makes you happy. And it's really nice when one of us is in a good mood."

Jackie walked to the first cabinet and took out the first file. "Where can I use the internet?"

"Um. My place. I don't have it connected here."

"Bob! What do you do?"

"For what? You know I'm always busy."

She shook her head. "Well, do you have a phone book?"

"Sure. Here." He pulled the thick white book out of a drawer. It bent into an arch as he handed it to her.

"I'd forgotten how heavy these are. How did we survive?"

"Stop complaining. Now let me work."

Jackie sorted through the last month's file for the orders. She found a folder and a hole punch and put them on the rings.

"What are you doing?"

"Making a customer file."

"How will I find them if I need to?"

"If they're orders, you'll know they're here."

"But I've got a system. It works."

Jackie raised an eyebrow, then started to laugh. "Sometimes you're so huggable. If you want I'll put them back when I'm finished. They've all got dates on. But I need them all together for now."

Bob grumbled, but went back to work.

To Jackie's surprise she enjoyed the repetitive task, taking each folder, extracting the orders, punching the holes, filing; then on to the next. It was soothing, especially as Bob's mood mellowed in the quiet. She went back four years, then opened the folder at the beginning again and sat down in front of the phone book. They all had names and addresses. Some of them had phone details as well. She found the first one that didn't and searched the White Pages. Harem, J. 24 Hawthorn St. Yes, here it was, a small miracle of analogue technology. There must be people all over the place still doing things this way. Weird. She moved on to the next one.

By one o'clock she was almost finished. Zach had texted back an hour ago. He was at his design course till three, she could meet him then.

"Fancy some lunch?"

Bob looked up and grinned. "Usually it's me asking you."

"I had a good week last week, I'll take you out. Where's nice?"

"I don't know. I've got my sandwiches."

"Leave them. We'll splash out."

"Some of the boys go to the Redwood Pub."

"Sounds a treat. Get your coat. And while we're driving, I've got an idea I want to tell you about."

8

Jackie waited for Zach on the steps of the Design and Arts College. He grinned wide when he saw her, his eyes sparkling. “You don’t usually call me. Usually I have to hunt you down.”

Jackie put a hand to her eye where an eyelash was digging in. She was preoccupied removing it for a minute or more, and by then there was no need to answer.

“What you been up to? You weren’t at the market.”

“Not much. Working for my brother. Got a new idea.”

“Do I want to hear?”

“Maybe. Actually, yes, it does have to do with you.”

“Me? How?”

“I want you to sell it for me. It’s not something I can do myself.”

“Why not? What can it be? What would you think I’d sell better than you? You’re always on about how hopeless I am, how I’ll never make a living. As if you’re one to talk, with that passive waif thing you’ve got going.”

“I make $3,000 most weeks of the season. And $10,000 last week. And that was only working a day at the market. How ’bout you?”

“You spend most of that on experiments.”

"Still. The fact remains. I'm a better salesman than you, whatever it may look like."

Zach looked at her, doe-eyed. A light smile played around his lips as she fired up. He put an arm out to her, steering her onto the pavement. His hand brushed her jumper, and he flexed his fingers as he brought them back to his side.

"So, what is it? What is it that I can sell that you can't? I'm intrigued."

"I could. Just not as well."

"Are you ever going to tell me?"

"Patience." She smiled a small smile to herself. Zach turned backwards as he walked to mirror her steps, peering down into her face.

"Come on!"

She laughed out loud. "It's almost worth not telling you. But I'm excited, I can't wait. Let me go back, to the theory behind it. You know I was talking about the poor, the disadvantaged, how a lot of their trouble, if you call it that ..."

"Violence, hunger, that sort of thing? I think we'd call it trouble."

"Yes, that, but sometimes it's not as dramatic as that. Sometimes it's just leaving one home before you've got another. And your friends don't have the sort of homes you'd just turn up at: they're full, you'd have to sleep on the sofa, and maybe their partners wouldn't like it. So you end up sleeping in the car, if you're lucky enough to have one, with one or two or three kids; or sitting at the bus stop wondering what the hell you're going to do now. I talked to them over the winter. They told me. They cackled and screamed through the stories, some of them, and others were ... ugh, haunted. Anyway, I asked them, and I got the stories, but I didn't get all I wanted. They could tell me what happened, physically, but mostly they really didn't have a handle on why." She shrugged. "I gave up, I lost interest when I didn't find the answer straight away. I should have stuck at it longer ..." Her gaze was far away, and she was silent.

"And ... I'm waiting for the payoff."

"Oh, Zach! You're so kind, so lovely. Would you wait, let me talk it through, get my thoughts in order?"

He threw his head back. "Okay, will-o-the-wisp, go on."

"Where was I? Yes, that's it. I began to wonder if the trouble was actually mostly impulsiveness, and if so, where that came from. What makes people impulsive or not impulsive? I think a lot of people who appear to be steady, fine citizens are just scared. They have the same impulses but their fear keeps them inert until the impulse has passed, and then society pats them on the back and calls them good people."

"You think they'd be better off if they jumped at random?"

"No. I don't know. Not at random. But following intuition. How did you know, for example, that you wanted to go to arts college?"

"God, that was easy. It was in my bones."

"And so you got the stall, did your sculpting, and sold your art. You see that's pretty special."

"I don't think so."

"Yes, it is. Lots of people think they want to be artists. But you knew, and you admitted it to yourself and you did something about it. So what makes you different? How did you know that strong gut feeling was different from a whim you could ignore?"

"You're not just talking about one idea here, are you?"

Jackie blinked, squeezing the top half of her face dramatically, then releasing it. "Just one idea? No, not now or ever, really. But the ideas go together."

"Well, can we separate them? I'm getting confused. On the one hand you've got impulses, and on the other you've got life purpose, a calling. Trusting my gut. Where do they intersect?"

"I want to know which of those impulses that some people follow and then mess up their lives, as society sees it, are real, important, and which are just garbage, better ignored. And I want to know whether the middle classes have the same set of impulses, and just treat them in a different way, or whether there is some fundamental difference."

"Okay. Clear. But why? Why do you want to know that?"

"Because I want to change the world."

Zach pushed out his jaw and nodded in large movements. "Of course. Knew that. But how?"

"That's where you come in. And I don't know. I don't know yet. I need more research. Way more research. And I want people to pay to be my subjects. That's why you need to sell it instead of me."

Zach was laughing now. "You left me way behind. Hold up!" He put both hands flat against his temples and rubbed them up and down, hard and fast. Jackie leaned forward eagerly.

"It was while I was going through my brother's files, through those suburban addresses, the kind of places where people buy a play frame for their kids and might still be there two years, four years, eight years on. I wondered, how could someone do that? What sort of impulses, what sort of intuitive nudges are they ignoring in order to reliably know they'll be in one place, one house, for that long? I can't make it make sense. So I want to test them. I've got an idea. It's not ready yet. I'll test it myself, and you can, and Bob. But I'm sure it will work."

"Okay. Now. Out with it. I cannot wait another second."

Jackie waved vaguely towards him. Her focus shifted outwards, as if the world had sped up and she had stayed at her usual pace. "I was thinking about the times when I move, when I go. One day I'm sitting outside my tent watching the waves, feeling content, and thirty minutes later I can be in the car, packed up and gone. So as I worked this morning, I felt through my body. I remembered some of those moments and I tuned in to what's happening, physiologically. Those moments are always super-clear for me. It's like slow motion, everything comes into focus and there's so much time ... So I was trying to work out, what it feels like. I imagined my blood in my veins, I imagined my eyelids blinking, I imagined the balletic movements of my arms. You know I can pack and roll at lightning speed. But at those moments, it feels slower, even though in fact it must be faster, because when I look at the clock again, almost no time has passed."

"So? So so so what?"

"I think if we put a wrist monitor on people, we'd be able to pick up those moments. I think we could make it reliable enough so that if we alerted them, got them to look at what they were thinking at those moments, they'd be able to learn something deep about themselves. I act on those moments. But a lot of people don't. What if we brought that into focus? It would change their lives ... What?"

Zach had pulled back, alarm on his face.

"What? What's wrong?"

"A goose walked over my grave. Something tells me this is dangerous."

"Don't be silly. How can it do any harm?"

"Didn't you just say, that acting on those impulses is what causes the problems of the underprivileged? And you're going to set that cat among the pigeons of the middle class?"

"Just as an experiment. If it doesn't go well we won't go on."

"But you're going to turn the pigeons into guinea pigs. Will you tell them what you're doing?"

Jackie's eyes narrowed. "Yes."

Zach mimicked her expression. "But you're not really going to, are you? You'll tell them something they won't fully understand."

"Well, but ... this is important. This could be really important. People might end up living their lives, fully and really."

"Don't you think that's for them to decide?"

"But if they just knew!"

"Jackie ... you know I love you. But think this through."

She looked away and swallowed. She blinked and screwed up her mouth, turned her face to the side, scratched her ear. "What was I saying?"

"I don't know what you were saying, not really. Think. Think carefully. You're a master of the thought experiment; take it to its logical conclusion theoretically before you act practically. You can do that."

"No I can't! Not with people. They often don't behave as I expect. I can't do it."

"Consider the possibility that you can. Observe. You're great at that."

"Well, but that's why I wanted to ..."

"Not with this contraption. Not yet. Observe real people, real lives."

"Well, that'll have to be the start of it anyway. I haven't made it yet. Then I'll test it myself first, then you ..."

"So you said."

"Sorry. I often repeat myself when I'm working something out." She looked crestfallen. Zach put his hand out to comfort her.

"Well, but okay, in theory, exactly what is it you'd want me to do?"

Jackie picked up immediately. "I'll make the device. It'll be just like a wristwatch, a sports watch, with a heartbeat monitor, maybe some conductivity testing mechanism, like a lie detector, to sense the physiological changes. Then it will beep when it detects a significant change of the sort we're looking for."

"And people will buy it, why, exactly?"

"That's the thing. It's a self-awareness kit. People aren't very good at being aware of their moods. This will let them know to pay attention. I read in a book that you can increase awareness of your moods by just setting an alarm every couple of hours and asking yourself what you're thinking and what you're feeling. If people wanted, we could set that simple kind of thing up as well. But because this is triggered by how people are actually feeling, it will let them know the critical moments. Then they text the information through to be logged on a website."

"A website."

"Sure. Otherwise how am I going to know?"

"For your experiment."

"Of course."

"And they'd do this why?"

"So we can help them."

"Aha." Zach nodded, as if agreeing, but his eyes were dull. "Let me know how that works."

"Well, we graph it for them of course. They log their mood, 1–10. A descriptor of the type of mood and what they were thinking. And the reading from the monitor. And once a week they come in for therapy."

"The therapist being ..."

"Well, me. That's why I can't be the one who sells them the device."

"I see."

"Well, that and it takes that special breed of sincere concern that you do so well and I can't usually muster."

"So. An unqualified therapist who can't muster the pretence of sincere concern."

"Not pretence! I didn't say pretence! Look, I haven't got it all worked out yet, okay? It's the start of a plan, maybe there's a simpler way. We can work it out together. But will you do it?"

"Of course! How could you doubt me?"

"You're teasing."

"I know. I'm sorry. Forgive me. It's been a long half hour."

9

Jackie paced back and forth through the campground trying to induce specific emotions and states in order to trigger her Mood Meter. The components were fairly straightforward: basic heartbeat monitor and conductivity meter, and a clock. The trick was in the programming – what proportional rise or fall in heartbeat indicated a dramatic change in state, and over what time? What type of change in skin surface sweat meant an emotional cause? The thing was useless while exercising – that was probably inevitable – or when there was a sudden change in temperature – she could live with that, it wasn't very common in the scheme of things.

But the sweat of fear, that was fascinating. Surprising, too; in retrospect the trigger was usually obvious, but often she hadn't been aware of it in the moment. And then there was that odd suite of symptoms reserved for seeing Zach – Jackie had to accept that she felt more for him than she had realised.

All well and good, but it was so slow, so frustratingly slow. Maybe now she was beginning to understand it she could simulate the feelings, train her thought in such a way that she could generate anger or sadness or impatience. Yes. She could do that. Just sometimes circumstances got in the way – she was happy about a new minor breakthrough and the black mood she had put so much effort into creating evaporated.

Zach appeared in the middle of the afternoon.

"I thought you might want to see this, so I brought it over." He looked around. "Campground's filling up."

"School holidays." She held out her hand for his Mood Meter. "Let me see." They walked companionably back to her tent to find her laptop. "So tell me, what was happening?"

To her surprise he blushed, pushing back the hair above his forehead and fluffing it by rubbing back and forth. "Well, I was working on a project, for my course, and it was awesome, I just got into this ... I don't know how to describe it ... I almost wasn't there – it was all coming easily, every idea following the last. And then it ... well, it got interrupted. The Mood Meter started doing that soft two-tone bleeping it does when you're starting to go to sleep. Which surprised me, you know, 'cause I was working hard and fast ... no, not hard, it was easy. But efficient. Super-efficient."

Jackie pointed to a place in the graphical display of the downloaded file. "Here?"

"Yeah, that's it. You can't see it so well because I only spiked into it for a couple of minutes, before I woke up to the sound. And then when I did, it was gone."

"Sorry. Hey, but do you remember what it felt like? It's like the alpha rhythm state, half-asleep, half-awake, that great state for learning. Do you think you could recreate it? Not the activity, just the state."

"I don't know. Yeah, I think so."

Jackie's face was eager. "Try."

Half a minute later, she bounced off the edge of her chair as the two-tone bleeping started again. "You did it! You did it! Wow! This is it."

Zach started a little and blinked as he returned to the present. "I did good?"

Jackie threw her arms around him. "Yeah, Babe. You did really good."

Her thoughts were sent spinning. Here was the value of it, here was the point. All those books talked about learning to be happy; here was the machine that made it real. Now Zach had shown the way, nearly everyone could do it. Imagine pre-set states like this! It was revolutionary. Choose your mood and set life going on that track. Fantastic!

10

Jackie turned as she saw a movement at the tent door. Mike was walking past, and glanced in. He had been avoiding her, and his face as she caught him was a picture of contradiction: curiosity and embarrassment; insecurity and defiance.

"Hey, Mike, come and look at this! I could use you for this experiment."

He looked for a moment in the direction he had been walking. Indecisive. Finally he stepped inside, hovering beside the wall, his eyes flicking from Jackie to Zach and back again.

"Hey, Mike," Zach said, coolly. Mike nodded.

"Here, come and look. This is amazing."

Mike approached in slow, hesitating steps, body turned sideways like a crab as if he were about to bolt for the door at any moment. He fixed his eyes on the screen where she pointed, where the graph of Zach's creative buzz was still on display.

"What is it?"

"It's a mood meter. It reads people's mood."

"How does it do that?"

"It measures physiological changes and states. Just simple. Then it alerts you when there is a change or when you reach a pre-set state you told it about before."

"How?"

Jackie held up her wrist. "Here. This measures heart rate and sweat - actually electrical conductivity. It's a little primitive - we could do more with breath rate and depth and level of oxygenation of the blood - but that's more invasive to measure and this does okay for a start. Show him the buzz again, Zach; I've set it, do it again."

Zach was staring at Mike, eyes dull. He didn't respond. "What's he doing here?"

Jackie looked rapidly from one to the other. Her mouth dropped open, then she pulled her lips in and pressed them closed.

"How you doing?" Mike said, feigning nonchalance. Zach continued to stare.

"You know I said he bought a whole Life-in-a-Box. He set it up next door. Whose did you think it was? No-one else has bought the whole thing."

"I assumed it was yours. Development or something. Why here?"

"It's a great spot," Jackie began, but Mike cut across her.

"I don't think it's safe for Jackie to be here by herself. Time someone started looking out for her."

Zach's fingers clenched on the back of Jackie's chair, scrunching the fabric, causing the uprights to flex inwards. Jackie's eyes rolled. "Shut up, Mike. I said I'm fine. Come look at this. Zach, do the buzz."

"Impossible. Can't do it. Don't know why." His voice turned with sarcasm like the sound of a car passing, Doppler effect souring the note.

"Well, but, okay, look at this. Tell him, Zach, tell Mike what happened." After the pause that followed, Jackie filled in herself. "Zach was working on a creative project and he's isolated the state of flow." She pointed at the screen. "See this pulse drop and the slow, steady rhythm." Mike peered at the screen with an expression that implied he knew exactly what he was looking at. "And here, see where it stops, blips up, then returns to the previous state." Her jaw came out and her teeth loosely brushed her upper lip. First one eye closed, then the other. Half a minute passed.

"Jackie?"

"Wait, I'm thinking." She turned her eyes up to Zach. "What do you think? We don't want the buzz killed by the alarm every time. Should we stop the alert? After how many times?"

Zach moved his shoulders to shut Mike out. "I don't know, maybe alter the sound, so you still know, but it's not so intrusive. Then switch it off once it's mastered."

"But it'd be different for negative states."

"Yeah, I guess. They should become less common but you'd still want to know when they happened and have them interrupted."

Jackie nodded. Mike's feet shuffled. "We need some way to input that. Maybe a multiple press of the reset button?"

"Yeah – one to stop now, and, I don't know, two or three. Two to alter the feedback sound, three to stop permanently."

"Sounds good." She opened another application and began typing.

Mike shifted his feet. "I don't know what the fuck you're both talking about. I'm going."

Jackie's arm shot out like lightning, grasping Mike's wrist. "No. I need you. I need some more subjects."

"Listen ..."

She fixed her eyes on his. His mouth gaped like he was caught in a cobra's stare. "I need you. Wait." After a moment she let go, continued typing, putting her hand out for a moment when he moved again towards the door, but only for a moment, without looking up, then resumed typing again. "I'll just be a minute."

She pressed enter then pulled down a menu to set the program compiling. As the spiralling wait signal spun on the screen she reached down to a bag on the floor next to her and pulled out another Mood Meter. She plugged it into the end of a cable running from a USB port on her laptop, then watched the progress bar as the new software downloaded. A satisfying descending scale indicated it was complete and she unplugged it, holding it out to Mike.

"Here, put this on." Zach laughed. Mike looked at the neon pink device with distaste.

"Haven't you got a ... I don't know, maybe a blue one?"

Jackie turned it in her hand with surprise, looking at it.

"He's got a green one, how bout that?"

"Sorry, this is the last one. I think the market is mostly women. I thought I'd try this and maybe something more subtle – baby pink, sky blue ... I don't know ... I ... I'm not that great at knowing how people will react." She tailed off, her expression crestfallen, then raised her eyes to his, pleading.

Mike sighed. "Okay, okay, give it to me. What am I supposed to do?" Jackie beamed. Zach crossed his arms and turned away.

Jackie picked up a notebook as Mike strapped the watch-shaped device onto his wrist, then placed it down on the table in front of her as she took his arm, standing and pulling him closer as she peered at the screen to check it was picking up his signals. "Your pulse is fast. Is that normal for you?" Mike swallowed. "You're sweating, too. Are you okay?"

Mike looked at her for a moment, then away. Zach's attention returned to them like he was magnetised. At the sight of Mike's embarrassment he sniggered. Jackie's eyes widened a moment then refocused on the screen.

"Anyway, here's how it works." Their hair was touching as they both looked at the tiny screen. Zach's foot began tapping. "You can read the measurements here. They reread every six seconds. The most important thing is when it beeps. That indicates a change, and it's the best time to get a correlation between thought and state. You write down the time in this book, what you were thinking, describe your mood and give it a desirability rating – 1:hate it; 10:nirvana. Easy." Mike nodded. "So it's beeping now. It's 11:32." She wrote it down. "What are you thinking?"

Mike glanced at her, at Zach, at the ground and swallowed. "I ..."

"Well, describe your mood."

"I guess I'm happy."

"And rating?"

"I'd say an eight."

"Great. So this is one you'd like to re-create?"

"Oh yes."

Jackie turned to the swishing sound of Zach leaving the tent. Mike took advantage of the angle of her face to lean in and kiss her.

11

A loud slapping sound fell flat against the fabric walls. Both Jackie's cheeks, and one of Mike's, glowed red. She took the book, picked up the bag from next to her chair and carried them across the tent, putting the book inside as she went. She leaned the bag near the entrance, then re-crossed and removed Mike's Mood Meter without looking at his face. His chest rose and fell rapidly. His mouth was open, his lower teeth exposed.

Jackie walked away to put the device back in the bag also. Next she unhooked her hammock and lay it on the ground. Seconds later it was packed small and rolled next to the table. Jackie moved a chair, set her laptop aside and tipped up the table. In her deft hands it became a box again, and over the next few minutes item after item of furniture disappeared into it.

Finally Mike spoke. "I'm sorry. Sorry. You don't have to leave." Jackie looked at him, her pale eyes slate grey. "Please. I'll behave."

Jackie shook her head, a momentary vibration, her nose flexing. "No, you won't."

"But ..."

Silence followed, with only the swish and click of the rolling, the carbon fibre rods reducing. A minute passed, then another. Jackie turned at the sound of the tent flap falling back. A few moments later a car started and its wheels spun, flicking gravel against the outside of the tent. She sat back on her heels, frowning thoughtfully. She walked over to where her bag had fallen sideways onto the floor. She looked inside. The book and the neon pink Mood Meter were gone.

Jackie sighed. She walked outside. Zach's car was still here but he was nowhere in sight. "Bugger." She stared into the distance for a minute, eyes unfocused, then returned to her packing, pulling down the tent and fitting it into the box also.

She fetched her box of supplies from the kitchen and once both boxes were loaded into the boot of the car she walked down onto the beach, shading her eyes against the glare as she looked along it. There was a speck in the distance that may or may not have been Zach.

Jackie leaned her head back and blew a sigh towards heaven. Hands in her pockets she scuffed her way back to her tent site, took a last look around her, got into her car and drove away.

12

This time she'd find somewhere different, somewhere she hadn't been before. She wound up the hills behind Oxford, on the edge of the Canterbury Plains, and pulled into a tiny, remote campground perched in an unlikely manner on the side of a hill. The next section over had been timber, newly logged. The smell of sap and decaying pine needles was strong in the air. There was no kitchen, only one toilet, one shower. Well, she'd cope. It was just what she needed, away from everything. Perfect.

She paid her money to the toothless grotesque on the desk. He wasn't old, maybe forty, but beaten and weathered by a hard life.

"Is there somewhere I can charge my laptop, my phone?"

"Only there." He indicated a power point underneath a stand of faded brochures. "Or since it's quiet you can have a powered site, and hook in there." Jackie took a minute to place the accent – familiar, but not common in this part of the world. Then she had it. Cornish. How had he ended up here?

"A powered site would be great."

"That'll be $12 extra then."

Jackie stared at him.

"Nah, don't worry about it, my Lovely, I was only joking." His ingratiating smile was not reciprocated. "All right, so take number twelve, at the top there. It's closest to the bathroom, as the crow flies."

Jackie nodded, knocking a farewell on the counter, digging into her pocket for her phone as she reached the door. From behind her came a cackle. "You can put that away. No signal for miles." Jackie stared back at him and the scratching giggle grated to a halt. "If you need to use it, go into Oxford. It's usually all right there."

Back in the car, Jackie slumped behind the wheel. Texting Zach would have to wait until later. Men. They were so emotional. She had barely enough energy to pitch the tent.

Half an hour later she sat at the table working out what she'd have to eat tonight. No fridge. No cooking facilities. Salami sandwiches, an apple; she'd forgotten the milk, left in the fridge at the other campground. She'd have to toss the bacon. "Damn you, Mike." She looked at her phone. Still no bars, no service. "And damn you, Zach. Why couldn't it have been you?"

Her own Mood Meter bleeped feebly, as it had been doing all afternoon. It needed charging. She slapped it into silence once more. It was still on the old software, so she couldn't silence it permanently. She blew out a sigh, reached for her book. "15:26. Thinking about Zach. Low. 2." As she looked up the list the last six entries were basically the same.

Jackie sat with her elbows on the table, fingers clutching her hair. She looked up at the sound of a voice.

"Oi there!" She stood and opened the tent to look down the terraced hill in the direction of the sound. There was the owner of the campground, struggling up the steps on crutches. The lower half of his right leg was missing, his trousers pinned haphazardly around the stump, and he was sweating with the effort of climbing.

"Hello?"

"Thought you might like some company," he wheezed as he finally reached her. "You seemed a bit depressed."

It was an offer it would be rude to refuse. "Come in. I'll make you some coffee." He hobbled in, whistling as he looked around. "This is very pretty. I've never seen anything like this before. Where did you get it?"

"I made it."

He looked at her with piercing blue eyes. "You don't say."

She felt awkward under his gaze and was grateful for the raucous cawing sound that drew her attention. She recoiled a moment later as a blur of feathers shot through the open flap. A red and green parrot settled on the man's shoulder.

"Hello there, my Lovely. Come back, are you?" He stroked the bird, clicking, then turned to Jackie once more. "Now. Introductions. This is Anna." The bird clicked in response, nodding its head. "How do you do?" it shrieked, holding out its wing.

"S'all right, you can shake it, just be gentle."

Jackie reached out tentatively, stretched so as to keep her body as far as possible from his as she briefly fingered the bird's feathers. "Hello, Anna. I'm well, and you?"

"Can't complain! Can't complain!"

"And I'm Craig."

"Hi, Craig. Jackie." She stared at his dirty outstretched hand for an awkward moment before shaking it. He nodded, as if the handshake sealed a contract. "So you invented all this. Just for yourself, or do you sell it?"

"I sell it, when I can, at the markets."

"That's not going to do you much business. You need the shops, proper distribution."

Jackie blinked her surprise. "Well, yeah, I know. But I wouldn't know where to start. And then I'd have to increase production. At the moment I make it all myself ... so I don't know."

"Well, I've got some contacts, I'll ask around. Now, did you mention some coffee?" He grinned, showing many gaps between a mixed assortment of teeth.

"Sure. Just wait a minute, I'm still setting up. Do you take milk? I haven't got any."

"It'll be fine without." He watched as she rummaged in a cylindrical bag on the floor, pulling out two telescoping mugs, a cafetière and a plug-in element.

"There's a bottle of water in the car, won't be a sec." She filled the cafetière with water and inserted the element, standing back with hands on hips to watch it boil.

"Mind if I sit down?"

She turned and only now seemed to register the crutches and the missing leg. "I'm so sorry. Of course. Please." She stepped forward to help but he had already pulled a chair back, leaned up his crutches and was hopping into position. He fell back onto the creaking fabric, causing Anna to flap for balance. He slapped the arms of the chair. "Comfortable, this.

We'd have a lot of buyers once people knew about it. Got any photographs? I could email it out to my list."

Jackie looked up, as if she could see through the tent walls. "A long list, is it? This is quite a small place." Bubbles formed on the element behind her.

Craig's eyes creased and his eyebrows twitched. "Argh! But I wasn't always here." He leaned forward, eyes fixed on hers. She fidgeted and looked away.

"I think I had some biscuits. I'll see if I can find them." She rummaged some more and slid open a packet of shortbread, placing the round plastic tray on the table between him. His eyes crossed as he stared hungrily at them. Jackie turned away. "Please, help yourself."

"Thanks, Lovely. This reminds me of home." Anna leaned forward and pecked at the piece in his hand. He broke off a corner and held it up for her.

The water was boiling now. Jackie switched off the element and took it out of the water, waving it through the air to cool it. She kept it in her hand as she stirred the coffee into the water, plugged in the plunger and placed it on the table. Craig sniffed loudly. Jackie watched in horrified fascination as his eyes rolled back, revealing a large expanse of white. "Don't that smell good! I haven't smelled anything like it since I got thrown out of that restaurant in town, and that was three months ago."

"What happened?"

"I sent my dinner back and they didn't like it."

"That doesn't sound fair."

Craig screwed up his face, trying to dislodge a piece of shortbread from between his teeth. He reached for another. "Well, maybe I could have tempered my language, but I was hungry, and I'd been waiting a while – now don't you go blaming them. I'm not complaining, really, just, I do miss the coffee, and yours smelled good and it reminded me ..."

Jackie pushed down the plunger and poured into his mug and then her own. She sat down opposite and took a piece of shortbread. She dipped it in her coffee. "So Craig, tell me about yourself."

"You want to know about my leg."

"Well ... I ..."

"It's all right to be curious. People are. But I won't tell you today. Not till I know you, and how you'll react. It's a hair-raising story, and you'll find it hard enough sleeping tonight."

"Why? I always sleep well."

He laughed. "Tell me that tomorrow."

Jackie pulled back as he laughed again. Her hand came down automatically to shut off the beeping of her wrist, but before she could get there, Craig had a grip around it, pulling it towards himself. "What's this, then? Another invention?"

"Yes," she answered, trying to pull away. He held tight, peering closely at it.

"I thought so. Now, tell me about this one. This one looks very wise."

Jackie gradually relaxed as she described the Mood Meter, gesturing wide with her free hand. Craig nodded sagely, eyes alternating between the face of the device and her own face, glowing now, and eyes shining.

"I can see that, I can see that," he repeated as she described her developing theories. "So why did it beep just now?"

Jackie shrugged. "You said about not sleeping well."

"And it scared you."

"I guess."

He laughed. "Well now, let's see if I can do it again." He roared into her face. Anna took off and Jackie flinched but the Mood Meter stayed silent. He leaped from his chair, mouth open wide, causing the table to totter. Jackie raised her eyebrows. Finally he brought his hands to her neck and his face to within an inch of her own. Now the device started beeping. He laughed again in triumph and let her go. "Not easily scared, though, are you?"

"Not easily, no. I lead a charmed life. But I'm not sure about you. Are you safe? Really?"

"Usually. Long as I like you."

"And you do?"

"I think so, Jackie, I think so."

He leaned back and took another sip of his coffee. Then he raised his mug. "I'll drink to safety if you will."

"I'd rather drink to friendship."

"Then that, too, Lovely, that, too."

INVENTOR

13

"So did you sleep then, Lovely?"

Jackie reared back as she exited the shower block, straight into Craig's chest. "You keep startling me," she commented as she collected together soap, toothbrush, toothpaste from the ground. "Is it intentional?"

"I s'pose so. I'm somewhat fascinated, to tell the truth. Most young ladies don't like me at all, but you're different. You don't seem to mind."

"I did, actually."

"What?"

"Sleep. Same as usual."

"I just thought, with the wind and everything."

"I like the sound of weather. It relaxes me." She turned and walked towards the path up the hill. Craig hobbled alongside. "What's up with you this morning?"

"Well ..."

"Yes?"

He was looking at the ground and she leaned in to interrupt his gaze. The corner of his mouth twitched up. "Would you have any more of that coffee? That was grand yesterday, I hadn't realised how I missed it."

"Sure. But that reminds me. Wait here." As she dashed back to the building she pulled a piece of folded plastic from her pocket. When she returned it was expanded, a water-filled bladder.

"That's handy."

"Yeah. It's way more practical than a jug: sealed, and only takes up as much room as the water it contains. I got it from a wine box. Only thing is they take ages to wash out and the tap's a bit narrow to fill through."

"Still ..."

"Still," she agreed. She slowed her steps to keep pace with him. "Where's Anna this morning?"

"I left her sleeping. Didn't want her to give me away when I surprised you."

Jackie's eyebrows arched.

"Do you want her? I can give her a call." He seemed eager to please. She nodded and immediately a piercing, tuneful whistle filled the air, followed by a crescendo of flapping wings. Anna circled Craig's head once, he lifted his arm for her to settle on and Jackie flinched as his hand came to rest on her shoulder. "Don't mind, now, I thought you'd like her."

Jackie stilled as she read his intention and Anna hopped from his fingers onto Jackie's shoulder, walking her feet: left, right, left, right, getting comfortable. Jackie's laughter pealed across the hillside. "That feels so weird!"

"But good, yeah? Friendly."

"Yes." She breathed in, large, and puffed the air out, cheeks beaming. "Come on, coffee's waiting."

As they sat drinking, Jackie leaned down to scratch her leg, one hand up steadying Anna, who had been pecking bits of shortbread from a plate Jackie held up. "Ever think about a kitchen, bigger bathrooms? This place could be so much more."

"That was the plan, when I bought it. I got it very cheap, because it's so small and simple. I got council approval, bought the land next door to expand once the logs were cut. I was going to do the work myself, but ..."

"The leg?"

"Yeah, the leg."

"So what about that, then? What happened?"

Craig stuck out his bottom lip and blinked.

"Come on. You know I can handle it."

"Well, actually it's not that exciting. I'd rather keep it to myself if it's all the same to you."

"No, come on. You promised."

"Well, all right. I'd not been here long, it was a couple of years ago. One of the old boys wasn't well and his dog went missing. I took the four-wheel motorbike to find him. I hadn't driven one much before. Well, I'd just spotted the dog when the bike rolled down a bank – pretty simple – and it landed on my leg. It was hours later they found me. And I lost the leg."

"But you said ..." She stopped herself. "Two years ago."

"Two years ago I could run, jump, laugh, just like you."

She gazed at him, eyes full. "It must be hard."

"It's hard not being able to walk, not being able to work, or even carry anything."

"Well, but what about an artificial one? At least you'd be able to do without the crutches."

"I ain't having a wooden leg. They call me pirate as it is, with the Cornish way of speaking and my lovely lady here." He gestured fondly to Anna, who nipped towards his fingers.

"Not wooden, of course not wooden. And no-one would know – there has been huge progress in prosthetics, natural movement, and super-light. You can even get specialised legs for different sports. The guy I get my carbon fibre and titanium from works with some manufacturers. With trousers, a shoe, you'd be running like a lad and no-one the wiser."

Craig tipped back his head and roared. "And the lads in the pub? They'd think it'd grown back on its own?"

"No, they'd know, of course, I just ... look, let me take you. This guy I know, he could really help you. Didn't they offer? At the hospital?"

"They did. I said 'no'. But they didn't describe it the way you have."

"Really, come with me."

"All right. If you think so ..."

"All right."

She nodded and reached out to top up his mug with the last of the coffee. As she did so, her Mood Meter beeped, a slow, gentle tune this time.

"Hey!" She smiled wide.

"What's that? That's new."

"I did it! I slipped into alpha state, I was thinking about something you said. This is great, I would never had known without the Mood Meter. 'Course I've lost it now, I'll need to turn it off."

"What is it?"

"For me, it's the state of ideas. An idea was forming."

"And what was it?"

"Just give me a minute. It was something about you – the leg, the coffee, the pub, the mower, Anna, the wooden/titanium leg. And this place. You want to make it bigger."

"Yes, but there's no money, and it's never full as it is."

"Well, let's do a deal."

"What?"

"I need somewhere to display my tents, and someone to show them, since I want to concentrate on the Mood Meter. You want to expand. It's beautiful here, people will come, you just need the facilities, and the marketing. Let's work together. I sell my complete packages with a year's lease on the site. You take a share of the profit. I help you set up a kitchen, better bathrooms. We'll be partners. And we get you fit, get you a new leg, so you can do everything you want to do."

He stared at her. "But really, why would you? Go into business with me? You'd be mad."

Jackie grinned. "No, I wouldn't. I know. I always know. I have an intuition for these kinds of things. It'll be great for me. Without having to go to the markets to sell the tents I'll have time to work on this." She held up her arm. Anna pecked at the coloured plastic and it gave a sick squeak. Jackie pulled it further away.

Craig stared at her wrist. "I been thinking about that."

"The plan?"

"No, that." He pointed at the Mood Meter. "I think I could do that. Help you test it. I'm not your average user, but I'd be variety. What do you think?"

"Sure. I'll have to make another one, but sure. Now, back to the plan. Shall we do it?"

"Expand? Together? This year?"

"You're tempted. Say yes."

He tipped his head on one side. His expression was flirtatious. Jackie looked away from his gaze. "And would that mean you'd be staying?"

"Probably. As long as it suits me. As long as you behave." She looked back. "You know what I mean? I'm not in the market for a boyfriend."

Behind his dark skin he blushed. He held up his hands. "I wouldn't dream of it."

"Then why did you look at me like that?"

"It's just my way, just my way."

"You like shocking people, disconcerting them."

He frowned. "I suppose so."

"Well then, Craig, that won't work with me, okay?"

"Okay."

"We'll get on fine. Don't pretend otherwise."

"And you'll take me as I am?"

"Of course."

"No 'of course', Miss! People usually don't."

"I can see that, Craig. But I will. I'm different."

"You certainly are."

14

Jackie's movements were stilted as she packed what she needed to drive into town. She knew she needed to go back to the market and she knew she needed more stock, but she wasn't looking forward to it. The complications of Zach and Mike were making her head fuzzy.

Today and tomorrow it would just be Bob and Sandra. On Saturday she'd have to face the others.

Craig hovered by the car, his face uncharacteristically still. He seemed lost in his thoughts. Jackie closed down the boot and turned. His eyes were on the ground, miles away.

"Okay. I'll be back on Saturday night, I think, depending on how the day goes. Sunday morning at the latest. Then we can start setting up the displays ... Craig?"

He looked up into her face, his expression sad.

"I'll be back."

He nodded half-heartedly, then shrugged.

"I will, look, I'm leaving all this."

He glanced around as she gestured at her tent.

"This is my home here. You believe me?"

His eyes met hers for a second, then slid away. "You'll be seeing these other guys: the one you like, and the one you say you don't. And your brother. Why would you come back when they are there for you?"

"Why would I say I will if I didn't intend to?"

"Intentions? Things change. Intentions are made of air."

"And this?"

He looked again at the tent. "This is real, I agree. Who knows? It might be enough. I'm not counting on it."

"Well, telling you isn't convincing you. I see I'll have to prove it."

"Coming back once doesn't prove it."

"Well, then, there's nothing I can do. You'll have to work it out yourself. Don't take too long, though, doubt is a waste of time and energy." She put out her hand and he tentatively took it. "Sunday."

He didn't answer, just looked away again.

As Jackie drove off the hill her phone began beeping: one, two, three, four, five text notifications, and still coming. She waited another ten minutes until the avalanche subsided then pulled off on a straight country road to see what they were all about. As expected: Zach, Mike, Bob. She read through them and texted back to Bob to ask if she could stay the next couple of nights, copying the messages to Sandra also. Then there was a phone message to say the rods she had ordered were ready. Lucky – she wouldn't have been able to build the stock she needed without them.

Zach's texts were confusing; she was pretty sure he wasn't saying what he meant. Oblique questions, a request for a mutual friend's number. She answered the simplest one, the final one: "Will you be at the market on Saturday?" with "I'll be there."

Mike's reports on the Mood Meter experiment she ignored, pushing them to the back of her mind where they festered. He was completely infuriating. She would have to decide how to deal with him.

Responses came from Bob and Sandra almost simultaneously: simple acceptance from Sandra, "where the hell have you been?" from her brother. She decided to drop in at his work to calm him down before she went to his home to use the workshop.

As she pulled back onto the road she thought she saw a flash of red and green in her mirror. "Anna?" She turned but there was nothing there. Thoughts of the bird and her owner followed Jackie all the way into the city.

She would have to work quickly to get two full sets of the Life-in-a-Box made in two days: one for the market, one for the permanent display she and Craig were planning. If she didn't sell one at the market they'd put them both up at the campground. Maybe they'd offer a reduced price until the new facilities were finished. How long would it take to build the new blocks? Calculations were flashing through her mind as she pulled into Bob's car park.

He was outside before she turned off the engine. "You said you were coming back to make those phone calls and design those tents."

She stopped short. "Oops. Sorry, I got distracted. I'll ..."

"You don't know when you'll do them, do you?"

"I'll fit some in this afternoon, and some tomorrow. But why don't you design the tents yourself? You'd enjoy it." She sighed. "I'm sorry. I didn't mean to let you down."

"It's okay, Sis, it's okay. Just tell me where you've been."

"Working on this new invention. And working out what it's for. And I've found a new way to market the Life-in-a-Box ... it's too long a story for now. How are you?"

Bob stared at her. "God, I wish I knew what goes through your head sometimes."

"It's not that complicated. I invent things. I look for ways to use them. I produce them, then I sell them. I try to make a living. It's fairly simple, really."

"But why? Why do you do that?"

She shrugged. "Because it's me, because it's who I am."

He stared, blinked, stared. "I can't keep up with it."

"It's a pretty simple rhythm. Pretty predictable. I could chart it for you if you like, make some projections."

"It's not funny. You disappear for days, I don't know what you're doing, where you are, even if you're okay."

"I'm always okay, Bob."

"So far."

"Always. Please don't worry."

He turned away. She followed him. "Bob ... is there something else?"

He stopped with his back to her. She watched his fists clench by his sides. "It's Sandra. I think she's having an affair."

Jackie froze mid-step. "What?"

His head shook side to side, the short hair static. “Forget it. Forget I told you. There’s nothing you can do.”

“Maybe not. But get in the car. Let’s go somewhere and talk.”

15

"So what's different?"

"She doesn't look me in the eye, for one thing. And then, in bed, you know ... she's distant. Then she'll be apologetic one minute, overly affectionate, and then gone again. She snaps at the kids, then cries with remorse. I have to ask her if she's thinking of leaving, but I can't, I just can't."

Jackie put a hand out to his. "Do you want me to ask her?"

He looked up into her clear eyes for the first time. "No. I have to do this. In my own way. In my own time."

"Well, do it soon. Uncertainty creates unnecessary scar tissue. You may be condemning her when that's not it at all."

"What else could it be?"

"I'm not the one you need to ask. But there are any number of things it could be."

"Like what?"

"I said, don't ask me. It will just set you off on more imponderable wild thought chases. Truth brings clarity, simplicity. Find out the truth. And do it soon."

As always happened when she worked, Jackie completely disappeared into the task of building the Box sets: tent, table, hammock, chairs, as well as all the bits and pieces, and pictures for the walls. As she worked, her mind projected future efficiencies, future enhancements. She needed to perfect the folding mechanism but for now the rolling style would do.

If she were creating more sets, it would make sense to block the work: do hammocks one day, chairs the next. The focus for now, though, was making two full sets, as quickly as possible. Once she was in the rhythm of it, her thoughts began to spiral out, through Bob and his situation, to Saturday's market, to a sighing pause on Zach, an exasperated glance at Mike, then further out to Craig, and the mystery he presented. For a while their joint plans flickered in her head, with a variety of possible outcomes, but then as she worked, his eyes became a lengthening second vision, mesmerising as a snake. She shook her head, pushed her hair back out of her face and continued working.

"You done?"

She looked up to see Bob in the workshop doorway, his face lined and tense. "No."

"Come inside anyway. I can't face it on my own tonight."

The mood over dinner was subdued. Instead of the usual gourmet preparation surrounded by vegetables the children had to be coaxed to eat, there were toasted sandwiches, bare on the plates. The boys began to complain, to question; a look and a movement from their mother silenced them, but after their eyes turned meekly down to their plates, Jackie saw Sandra's face fill with sadness and guilt. She stood quickly from the table, leaving her untouched meal to return to the kitchen. Bob's eyes turned to Jackie, in them begging desperation. She pushed back her chair and followed Sandra out.

"Hey. Can I help?"

Sandra managed a weak smile as she assembled ingredients for the next round of sandwiches. "Suddenly developed some culinary expertise?"

"I didn't necessarily mean with the food."

Sandra looked at Jackie and her eyes filled with tears. "Actually there is something. Are you going to be here tomorrow?"

"Yes. And tonight, if that's okay. I have a lot to do before Saturday."

"Then I know it's a lot to ask, but would you take Clara for a couple of hours in the morning?"

"Of course."

"I can't tell you why."

"I don't need to know why. I'm happy to take her. But I think maybe Bob ..."

"No! I don't want to ask him. Please, tomorrow? Around nine?"

"Of course." She held out a plate for the sandwiches Sandra was removing from the toastie maker and watched for a moment longer as the next ones were prepared. "I'll take these out, shall I?" And as Sandra, lost in thought, didn't answer, she turned and left the room.

At midnight she felt her eyes pulling closed and over the next hour she had to correct more than one mistake. She should go to bed, start fresh in the morning. She would have to work fast to get everything done.

She passed through the kitchen, finding Bob at the table, his head hanging over a cup of cold tea.

"Couldn't sleep," he said as she sat down beside him.

"What happened?"

Again, that look that made her heart thud in her chest.

"Nothing happened. Nothing at all."

The device on Jackie's wrist started beeping, eerie in the deep of night. She slapped it, silencing it, then removed it. There were times when sadness was appropriate, when knowing about it didn't help things at all.

16

Jackie always enjoyed spending time with Clara. There is something so easy about pre-verbal babies, if you will just let go and adjust to their rhythm. She could look into Clara's eyes forever, mirroring her expressions, generating helpless laughter with a simple, deeply engaged game of peek-a-boo. The two hours passed like a minute and before Jackie was aware, Sandra was lifting Clara off her knee into a tight, desperate hug. Jackie stood, instinctively reaching out her hand as Clara began to cry.

"Sandra, for God's sake, what is it?"

Sandra closed her eyes tighter. Tears rolled down the side of her face.

"Sandra?" Still no answer. Jackie leaned back, closed her own eyes and reached out for Sandra with her heart and mind. Immediately a black cloud engulfed her, darkness descending like a choking fog. Jackie's eyes sprang open. "Oh my God! You're not being unfaithful. You're sick!"

"Oh Jackie! Please help me. I don't know what to do."

"Tell me what's happening. What is it?"

"Nothing's definite yet, nothing's confirmed. They want to do more tests."

"And to start with? How did this start?"

"Just routine. Just a routine smear test. It came back suspicious, and they asked me to come in for another one. I had this horrible feeling, this horrible certainty that this was it, this was me, over. I went into a spiral. I tried to tell myself it would be okay, I would be okay, but I couldn't shake the feeling of dread. God, my children. How can I leave my children?"

Jackie took her hand, staring open-mouthed into her anguished face. "Darling!" Sandra made as if to twist away, but then she gripped Jackie's hand and pulled her to herself with sudden force. She gripped around her with a tight arm hold, Clara wriggling and struggling on the other side. Clara's cry had quietened to a panicked whimper. Jackie pulled her own arms out of Sandra's embrace and wrapped them around mother and child, holding them until Sandra began to relax. Jackie pulled them towards the sofa and they all collapsed onto it.

A lengthy silence followed. Clara climbed down onto the floor and crawled away across the room. Jackie watched her as she came to a stop, flipping into a sitting position with her mother's car keys in her hand. The car alarm blipped repeatedly as she turned it on and off. Her head turned towards the sound with delighted interest and she pressed the button again.

"But you said, there's nothing definite," Jackie ventured. "Are there any symptoms?"

"No."

"So it could be nothing."

"It could be. That's what I keep telling myself. But somewhere inside me, I've decided it's true, the very worst it could be is true."

"You know that's not good for you. It won't help, and it could make things worse."

"I know! But I can't shake it."

Jackie hesitated. "And Bob. You haven't told Bob."

"I can't! How can I? He'd be so worried. And he wouldn't know what to do. There's nothing he can do. He's better not knowing. It's better if I keep it to myself."

Jackie took her time over her next breath, choosing her words. "Do you really think you can keep it to yourself? It's obvious there's something wrong."

"To you. But you're a woman; women have a keener sense of these things."

Jackie frowned. "Sandra ..."

"What?"

"You're ... you're not as good at hiding it as you think. He knows something's wrong. He's tearing himself up imagining what it is. You have to tell him."

"I can't! I just can't. I can't tell him I'm going to die."

Jackie looked at her sister-in-law. Somehow it was worse that she was usually so phlegmatic. Some people thrive on drama, but Sandra was in a nose-dive, seconds away from a disastrous crash.

"And you have to calm down."

"How? How!"

Jackie pulled her face around and fixed her with her eyes. "Stop it! Just stop. Look at me. Take strength from me."

She could feel Sandra's face shaking in her hand, but she held her gaze, willing calm into her own heart, watching emotion after emotion parade through Sandra's eyes: terror, grief, panic, confusion; then, after two long minutes, her expression began to clear, her face began to mirror Jackie's calm. Her breathing had been shallow and fast, interleaved with periods of held breath. Now she exhaled fully and paused momentarily before the next inhale. There was a hiccough or two, then silence.

"Okay now?"

"Okay, for the moment."

"What can I do? What can I do to help?"

"There's nothing to do. Just wait for the results of the tests I had today. Three weeks. Three long weeks. How am I going to make it through?"

"You will. And I will help you. There's no point catastrophising. It's important you stay calm. Now let's make a plan. What would help? What would need to be done if the worst happens? You might feel better, more able to be optimistic, if you knew some of that stuff was handled."

"I don't know. I don't know." Sandra began to shake again, her arms fluttering around in the air away from her body. "What will happen to the children, who will look after the children, if I'm gone, even if I need treatment?"

Jackie took her hands again. "I'm here. I can look after them."

"But you love your freedom."

"I love my family."

"And you're so ... impractical. How would you cope?"

"I'm great at solutions, I'd find my way. And I won't need to. You'll be here. We're just talking contingencies, unlikely contingencies. Bob's here, and me. They'll be with people they love." She watched as Sandra's shoulders dropped a little, and some of the tension left her. "What else?"

"Well ... there's the house, I guess, but ..."

"The house will be fine, you know that. It's the people that matter. Bob, the children and you."

"Yes. And it may not be anything, anything at all."

"That's right."

"But how will I remember that? The panic, it happens so fast. And then it's like I'm gone." She got up and began to pace. Jackie stood, too, as if to stop her. She swayed gently on the spot in time with Sandra's pacing, and gradually Sandra slowed to a stop.

"I think the first thing is, you have to tell Bob. Or if you really can't, let me. He can help you, I know he can. You just have to tell him what you need."

"What do I need? How can he help?"

"You need his arms around you, to calm you down when you can't do it yourself. You need his steadiness. And then beyond that, you need something else to think about, something to take your mind off this. Fixating on it and fretting, it's not healthy. If there's something to do, do it. Otherwise do your best to forget it."

"But I can't! I can't!"

"You can, and I can help you. But first, Bob. Are you going to tell him, or am I?"

17

Bob stared at Jackie, relief rolling down his face in waves. "She still loves me. She isn't leaving."

"No."

Then his eyes tightened. "But she might be sick."

"And she might not be. She doesn't know anything at this stage. But she's panicking. She needs you to stay calm. Can you do that?"

He looked up at her, unable to suppress a smile. "She loves me. I can do anything."

"Okay. Then go home. Put your arms around her. Hold her till she's calm. I've promised her that if anything happens, if she needs treatment, if ... well, that I'll help you with the children."

Bob looked at her. His face fell as the terrible possibilities in front of him sunk in.

"Bob. Stop. You don't know anything. Hope for the best."

Still he stared at her. "She might ..."

"This is just it. For both of you. You have to hope for the best, keep telling her. Get a grip. Keep hold of yourself."

His eyes widened. Slowly he nodded.

"Whenever you don't know what to do, just hold her. Stroke her hair. Concentrate on making her calm. And for when you're not there, give her this." Bob looked down at the green Mood Meter Jackie held out. "It's mine. I'll make myself another one. The panic sets in before she knows it. This will let her know, remind her to get help, call someone, do whatever it takes to calm herself down." He stared at it without moving. "Please, Bob. Take it. It will help." Slowly he reached out his hand and took it, staring at it dully. "When it beeps, she can press this button to get it to stop. Then she should call someone – you, me, anyone else you can think of – to talk her through it. Once she gets better at it, she may be able to handle it herself, with a cup of tea, something simple. But to start, she should call someone. Are you listening? Tell me what I said."

"Press the button. Call someone."

"Right. Great. Now go home, spend the day with her. I'll be in the workshop, and tomorrow at the market, just a phone call away. Then I need to go back out to Oxford, but I'll do what I need to do and come back. Three weeks, they said, till the test results come back. I can be around that long, if you need me."

"Thanks, Sis. Thanks." He frowned. "You're good at this. So calm. So sane. When did you get so ..."

"Practical?"

"Well, yeah."

Jackie laughed. "You guys! What do you think? How do you think I've survived all this time?"

"But you're usually so ..."

"I'm not like you, I know. But give me some credit, please. Now go."

18

Jackie worked late into the night getting everything ready for the morning. It never occurred to her that she could slow down, skip the market this once, make things easy for herself. She had a plan, she stuck to it, regardless of new factors that came into play.

As she worked, images and memories spun in her mind: the sense of panic, all the more disconcerting because Sandra was usually so placid; Bob's relief, out of place and selfish but understandable; the thought of seeing Zach tomorrow, and Mike; and Craig, planning what to say to Craig, disoriented by the uncertainty that her offer to Bob and Sandra created.

Towards dawn she put the last items into the new boxes. She had unconsciously altered course around midnight, putting together chair after chair, lulled by the easy familiarity of building her long-term best-seller. It had taken a jolt of consciousness around two to put her back on task and complete the boxes.

She took out her phone to look at the time. 5:40. No point going to bed now. She didn't think she could sleep anyway, and she needed to be at the market at nine to set up. It would be horrible doing that in the stickiness that came from pulling herself out of two or three hours' sleep. She tipped back her head, feeling her shoulders creak. From habit she glanced at her wrist, but she had given her watch – her Mood Meter – to Sandra.

Well, why not make another? That would at least be something to do. She rooted through a box of components, pulling out a blue casing. She smiled. Mike would be happy to swap. It was time to forgive him.

"Zach, hi!"

Zach looked up from where he was placing stock, arranging his clay sculptures, and looked away.

Jackie stepped in front of him. "I looked for you. Where did you go?"

"For a walk. That was a week ago. You didn't look very hard."

"It's so confusing."

"What is?" His voice was truculent, but his face showed reluctant interest.

"You." He grinned. "And Mike." The grin soured. He turned away again. "You know I'm not interested in Mike."

Zach's eyebrow raised. "He's interested in you."

"So?"

Zach's head tilted.

"Well? So?"

"I don't ..."

"I'm not interested in him. I like you. But you have to take me as I am – vague, distractable."

"Indecisive."

"Really? You think I'm indecisive? What makes you say that?" Jackie's face was full of curiosity.

"Now there, you see! Straight off the topic again."

"But I'm just responding. Responding to what you said." Her forehead creased. She held out a hand towards him. "I don't like this uncertainty."

"What uncertainty?"

"Are you going to ask me out or what?"

Zach bit his lip. His eyes moved to the left. "Um ... Well, would you? Go out with me?"

"Yes, Zach."

"I mean ..."

"Yes?"

He gulped, coughing, then recovered. "I mean, be my girlfriend?"

"Yes, Zach. That'd be nice."

"Oh." His chest puffed forward. "Well ..."

"I'm going back to Oxford after the market. There are some things I need to sort out. Want to come?"

"Yeah. Really? Yeah."

"Okay. Get selling. It's a day to celebrate."

She opened the first box and with a few efficient movements expanded out her stall tent. Table, display photographs and samples followed. Within two minutes she was sitting in her chair, moved forward to watch as Zach continued unwrapping and arranging his pieces.

"That's new." She pointed to the long, thin figure of a woman, serene and simple. "I like it."

"Yeah." Zach leaned forward and his hair fell across his face. "It's you."

"Wow. Me?"

"I remembered that thing you said, about the lake, the reflection in the lake. Here, let me show you." He pulled out a wide, shallow dish, glazed black on the inside, and took a bottle of water from the ground, pouring it in up to the level of the glaze. He placed the figure into the water, the base lifting it so the feet stood precisely on the surface. A perfect reflection was created, the dish shaped forward of where she stood. "It's how I think of you."

"Sweet."

"Well, you know, how you take your time, you always wait before you respond to things. I can always trust you. Your world reflects what you want it to. That's what it means."

"I'm flattered." They both stared at the sculpture. As they did so, there was a rumble, a large truck passing. The surface of the water broke up, rippling with randomly interconnected bouncing waves. Jackie laughed. "Well, we're none of us perfect. That's the joy of life."

Zach's face had fallen into disappointment at the breakup of his image. He looked up into Jackie's eyes and relaxed into an echo of her laugh.

19

Jackie drove with the sound of Zach's burbling voice in her ear. She smiled from time to time at the effusion of his happiness, the transparency of his excitement. He had sold the first Lake Woman sculpture, and with a small degree of embarrassment, unwrapped another. "I thought you said I was unique," she teased.

"I can't believe I sold four. People love them. You are my angel of luck. I've never sold four of anything on one day before. I thought I might have to give up the stall, some weeks I was barely breaking even, but of course I didn't want to stop going ... and now, I don't know how I know, I just feel it, this is the start of real success for me." He chattered on and on as they crossed the Waimakariri Bridge and turned off the motorway onto the long straight road that would take them most of the way to Oxford. Jackie turned on some slow jazz, winding the volume back to almost nothing. Zach's voice gradually altered speed to match it, his enthusiasm slowing to a more measured pace, the smile still wide on his face.

They paused in the township, Jackie contemplating a stop, a coffee, more chat before encountering Craig, but after only a brief moment of hesitation she turned into the side road that would take them home.

The car settled with a final gravel-crunch next to her tent. For a moment she stared out over the plains, looking for the glimpse of the sea in the distance. The air was hazy today after the clear view earlier in the week, and she could only imagine she could see water.

Down by Craig's hut a figure appeared. She got out of the car and waved. Cupping her hands to her mouth, she called out, "We'll come down. Wait there," but the thin edge of a crutch waved in the air and he began hobbling towards them.

Jackie turned to Zach. "Okay. Here's the thing. I haven't told you about Craig."

Zach's mouth opened. Before he could speak, his question was stopped by a flurry of wings, a red and green blur.

"It's too much to explain all at once. Just trust me. Listen, you'll figure most of it out, and I'll tell you the rest later. I made plans before we ... got together. And before ... well, I haven't told you about Sandra, either. There'll be some adjustment. Just stay calm."

"Hey there!" she called.

"You said you'd come back, and here you are!" Craig let out a cackle of delight. "I doubted you, and look!" He slowed a little towards the end of the last steep flight of steps, then accelerated again as he reached the flat ground of the terrace. "Hello! Hello! You've brought someone with you."

Zach took Craig's outstretched hand with trepidation.

"Craig!"

"Zach."

"Pleased to meet you. Isn't she something, this little beauty? She's a clever one, no mistake. We're in business, aren't we, my Darling? Did she tell you?"

"I was just about to."

"And how did it all go? Did you get everything done, did you sell anything at market?"

"I did fine, but I've still got both box sets for display, so that's great. Zach and I will put them up this afternoon. There may be a delay, though, with the rest of it. It's my sister-in-law. Here, come in, I'll make us a coffee and we can talk."

Jackie turned to Zach as Craig crunched back down the hill again. She stood with her back to the door flap, eyes fixed on Zach's as he sat still at the table, his mouth hanging open as he processed the information overload.

"Jackie ..."

"Later."

"But ..."

Their eyes stayed locked and Zach's mood shifted. Jackie's eyelids fluttered shyly downwards. "Come here?"

She heard his chair slide back over the fabric of the tent floor. His feet appeared in her line of vision and she felt a hand on her waist. Her Mood Meter beeped. She took it off and reached up to hang it on a hook by the door, tuning in to the raw feel of her heart inside her chest.

He pulled her to him. "I've dreamed of holding you for so long. It seems like ..."

"What, Zach?" she breathed.

"Like a miracle," he whispered, and he leaned down to meet the lips that were rising to his.

20

Jackie woke to see the swaying of a second hammock tilting her field of vision. Ah, Zach! The memory flooded through her and she squirmed with pleasure, sending her own hammock into a disorienting wave. She squeezed her eyes shut and smiled a smile her face could barely contain. He was so shy, so awkward, so perfect. Her body had been ready for more, but her mind was running to catch up. First boyfriend at twenty-one. Well, he had been worth waiting for.

She tipped herself expertly onto the floor and slipped a pair of jandals onto her feet, pulling a cardigan around herself as she stepped out into the spring morning. She gazed out over the plains as she skipped down the stairs. Even the trek to the toilet block was magical this morning.

When she got back, he was sitting, bleary eyed, at the table.

"How do you sleep in those things? It was like being at sea." She danced over near enough that he could reach up and kiss her cheek. "Ah, yes, good morning."

She smiled and blinked, slowly. "Coffee?"

"Yes, please."

"And cereal for breakfast? It's only UHT milk."

"Divine."

She sat opposite him, mesmerised, as he drank his coffee from a bowl. She sucked orange juice from a TetraPak, with a straw.

"So what's the plan for the day?" he asked, once he had come fully awake.

"I just need to get the display tents set up, really. We'll go back through the plans for the extended facility blocks so I can start arranging building materials. A couple of hours and we can head back to town. I want to check on Sandra, see that she's a little more stable ... and I need to meet with Mike." Her lips came out in an exaggerated pout as she watched for Zach's reaction. As predicted, his face darkened into a frown.

"Why?"

"He said weeks ago he had someone to help me market my tents. I want to talk to them, and he hasn't given me their name. He said he would."

"When? I thought you weren't talking to him."

"Why would you think that?"

"Because you left. You ran away. To get away from him."

"He broke my trust. I wouldn't live in a tent next to him any more. I still won't. But I can talk to him. I'm not resentful. I spoke to him yesterday."

"When?"

She stretched her mouth out, shook her head. "Just during the day."

"I didn't see him come to your stall."

"He didn't. He wouldn't, actually, said he wouldn't dare. So melodramatic! I went to see him. I wanted to swap the Mood Meter he was wearing, ask how it was going." She reached up to the hook by the door to take down the pink device. She held it out to show Zach, then put it on. "He said he wanted a blue one, so I made him one."

Zach grunted. "I don't think you should talk to him."

"What would that achieve? I don't want him kissing me without my permission. I don't want him living next door. But we're friends."

"He's an arsehole."

"So?"

"What do you mean, so?"

"I mean, why does that matter? I set my boundaries. Apart from the jerky behaviour, I like him, he's refreshing ... oh, settle down!" Her face crumpled, near to tears. "I don't understand people, so inflexible, so hypocritical! We all have faults. Why do people pretend they don't?"

"Oh, Jackie, don't cry, please. But some faults are worse than others."

"Other people's faults – that's what you think, isn't it? Your own faults are okay, understandable, forgivable, but other people's aren't. I've noticed that logic so many times before, and I don't get it. It doesn't make sense."

Zach looked at the ground, confused. "I didn't say my own faults are okay. I hate them, but ..."

"What, Zach? I don't understand."

"He's not safe. I want you safe."

Jackie put a fist to her chest. Her face squeezed, features compressing. She stood and walked around the table to where he sat. "I'm always safe, Zach. Just, I'm not always happy, when the people I love don't get along."

"You love him?"

"Not the way I love you, of course. But yes, that's the way I feel about everyone I care about. I have to call it love, because of the way it sits inside me."

"Even when someone is so ... exasperating."

"Even then. Don't I exasperate you sometimes?"

"Oh yes."

"And does that change the way you feel?"

"No. It's part of the reason I love you, because you are the way you are."

"Well, exactly. And I know how to protect myself from people's faults, because I see them clearly, because I'm not tied up with condemning them for those faults, and justifying the condemnation."

"Still ..."

"What?"

"You've bamboozled me with your logic, but I still don't trust him around you."

"Or me around him?"

"That's not what I ..."

"Then just come with me, see how it works. I keep hold of myself. Trust me. Don't ask me to throw people out of my life."

Zach nodded and looked up into the corner. Jackie watched as he breathed slow, wondering what was going through his mind. "It's a new way of thinking, accepting people."

"I don't know. I guess so. It just makes sense to me."

His face twitched. "And if it's all true ..." He seemed to be speaking more to himself than to Jackie. "There's someone I'd like you to meet."

21

Jackie felt a momentary pang of foreboding as she drove out of the campground. She glanced into the rear vision mirror, but Craig had already disappeared into his hut. He hadn't been happy about her leaving; he said he wanted to get moving on their plans.

"It will happen soon enough. Have faith." But he had just looked doubtful. Zach was also brooding darkly. She felt as if she was carrying the world all on her own.

She looked across to where Zach sat, head leaning on the window strut, silent words forming on his lips. Her heart constricted in her chest, and she felt unsettled, uncertain. Just put one foot in front of the other. Keep going. It will all turn out. Her wrist beeped and Zach looked up, concern erasing his self-absorption.

"What? What is it?"

"I don't know. Something. I don't know what. Everything feels up in the air, I don't know what's going to happen."

"Oh."

"Forget it. That's life. We don't control it. Just sometimes that feels okay, and sometimes it doesn't. Sometimes it goes approximately to plan, and sometimes everything is a surprise. I guess I've just reached the limit of my calm unconcern."

"What are you worried about?"

"Sandra, I guess. And going into a new phase of business."

Zach sat silent, biting his top lip.

"It's okay. A momentary glitch. I'll handle it. It will all be fine." She repeated the phrase to herself, silently, two or three times, then nodded, and pressed down on the accelerator, taking the car up to the speed limit.

"Bob, Sandra? It's me."

She found them in the living room, gaudy children's television playing in the background. The three children were sitting on the floor and Bob and Sandra were intertwined on the sofa, smiles on their faces.

"Hey! The prodigal. We've been waiting, we wanted to thank you."

"What do you mean? I've been away one night. Thank me for what?"

"This thing. It's been a life-saver." Sandra held out the Mood Meter. "You can have it back now, I've got myself under control."

Jackie waved it away. "You keep it. You might want it again."

"I don't know what happened, I had lost myself. It was terrifying. But having this to pull me back each time, it worked an instant miracle. And Bob, he's been terrific." She turned to her husband with an adoring expression. "I'd forgotten what an angel he is." She put her hand on Bob's leg and moved it upwards in a way that made Jackie feel she should leave the room.

Bob blushed and grinned.

"So you don't need me, then?"

"We're glad to see you. But we're fine."

"Well, then, I'll ..." Jackie turned back towards the kitchen. "Hang on."

Back on the doorstep she looked out to the car, waving at Zach to come in. She took him by the hand and led him through the house.

"Since all's well here, there's someone I'd like you to meet."

Zach sat watching as Jackie worked on more stock, steadying herself with the familiar tasks, making intermittent conversation.

Finally Zach's impatience broke through. "There must be something I can do, something I can help with."

She looked up, gazed around her as if she had forgotten where she was. "Maybe. I've got so used to working alone."

"I can't sit here doing nothing."

"Well ... here, you could stitch these. You see the markers? Seat and back. That'd be great, then I can put them together.

She pulled a set of rods off a shelf, selecting several different lengths and connectors, watching and waiting as Zach worked on the last seam. His Mood Meter beeped. "Can you not watch me? You're making me nervous."

Surprised, Jackie turned away. "That's weird. That's something I hadn't thought of." Curiosity pulled her back again, and she peered even more closely over his shoulder.

"Glad to be a useful guinea pig," he said, teeth gritted. The beeping started again.

"Oops, sorry."

"It's okay. I'm done now."

He handed her the completed fabric sheets, looped over to accommodate the rod structure. He watched as she clipped it all together, rolled it and put it in the box with six others. "You're really good at that."

"Thanks." She turned, freezing as she realised how close he was. "And thanks for the help." Her head tilted slightly, and his lips dropped down onto hers. Both Mood Meters started up, slightly off key from each other, a cacophony.

"Here." Zach removed hers and then his. "Time for a little aural privacy." He put the Mood Meters in his pocket and leaned down again, wrapping his arms around her, humming appreciatively into the silence. A few delicious minutes passed.

"Don't let me interrupt."

"Hi, Bob." Jackie looked at the ground to avoid her brother's delighted grin.

"Just wondered if you'd like lunch. But maybe later. You look like you've found another way to satisfy your appetite." He sniggered. Zach joined him.

"Shut up, both of you. Boys!" She took Zach by the hand and as she walked inside she adopted a sexy hip swagger that silenced them both.

22

Jackie sat opposite the very urbane businessman, with Mike at her right-hand side. This man was not at all what she had been expecting – Mike had described him as a shark but he seemed perfectly pleasant.

"How's your mum, Mike? Still coming up with those gorgeous designs?"

Jackie turned to Mike as he shuffled his feet under the table. "Yeah. She's still doing well." Jackie combed her memory for Mike's last name. There was a fashion designer who matched it.

"Sheila Flamank? She's your mother?"

Mike nodded. Mason smiled wolfishly. "I knew her when she was at university. God, she was gorgeous, I should have snapped her up when I had the chance. But I missed out. Your dad still in the picture?"

"Off and on. You know Mum, always likes a bit of drama."

"Yeah, maybe that's where I went wrong. Too dull, me. But a man can dream."

Mike cleared his throat, embarrassed. "So what about Jackie, then? Can you help her?"

Mason looked through Jackie's promotional images for the third time. "And all this fits in this box?" He indicated the sample on the table.

"Yes."

"And you're selling currently where?"

"Just at the markets, and just what I can make myself. I'm in the process of setting up a permanent display, out at Oxford. We'll have a website. Then we can sell all over the world. But it's down to what I can manage by myself. The production takes a lot of my time, and now there's this new project I'd like to be focusing on."

"Can production be automated?"

"Streamlined, definitely, but it would still need people for assembly."

"But with facilities, with funding, you could step it up."

"For sure."

He sat back. "It's not my area, but I can see great potential. And I'm in the mood for a bit of diversity, a bit of variety. Why not? There are the obvious ready-made markets, camping shows, recreational groups. And I think there's something else, a new market we can create. Have you heard of downshifting?"

"No, what's that?"

"It's the new trend to re-think life, to work out what's important, to take a step back. It's just brewing, but I have an idea that we can create a community, and sell to the downshifters. Sell the romance of the nomad's life – hey, what about this! Could you redesign the box to be a suitcase? Imagine being able to travel the world with your life in your luggage!"

Jackie looked at the box on the table, mentally reconfiguring the proportions into a classic case shape. "Yeah, I think so. Easy."

"And how much does it weigh?"

"11, 12 kg. Something around that."

"So with a 20 kg allowance there would be room for clothes and everything, even for one."

Jackie grinned. "It's so refreshing to talk to someone who really gets this. I'm so used to being the only one excited."

"Sure. Look, let me get my head around it, come up with a possible company structure. You said you had a new project, so you'd prefer to be less than full time with this?"

"Yeah, if I can. The new idea has lots of possibilities, I'm just seeing the tip of the iceberg at the moment."

"Tell me!"

Jackie hesitated. "Aren't we best with one thing at a time?"

"Does it tie in? How does it fit with the Life-in-a-Box?"

"Not specifically. Not in any obvious way, except ..."

"What?"

"Except somehow I have the same feeling about both. They're completely different concepts, but they're both about freedom. This give you physical freedom, freedom of place. The new device gives you emotional freedom. Emotional awareness, first, then that leads to choices, and that, for those brave enough to follow it, leads to freedom."

"Fascinating! Tell me!"

Jackie puffed out her cheeks. She could feel Mike jiggling at her side. Instinct told her it was too early. She sat back. "Okay. Mike, tell him what you know. I'm still thinking."

Mike leaped up and ran around the table, shoving his arm in front of Mason's face. Mason looked like he feared he was being attacked, but he held still, assessing the situation.

"Here!" yelled Mike, waggling like a recently sprung jack-in-a-box. "This is it! The Mood Meter. It measures your moods and beeps to let you know how you're feeling."

"But don't you know how you're feeling?"

"If you think about it, yes. But if you're concentrating on something else, no. And when people go into negative states – angry, sad, scared – they have a tendency to go absent, disappear cognitively. This thing beeping can bring you back, bring you conscious, so you can deal with whatever's happening in a powerful way."

Jackie stared. Mike's use of language indicated a deeper understanding than she'd thought he was capable of.

Mason shook his head. "I don't quite get it."

Mike threw back his head and laughed. "That's just it! No-one does. You can't imagine the power of it till you've tried it."

"Well ..." Mason turned to Jackie. "Is that true? Does it need to be experienced to be believed?"

Jackie continued staring at Mike. "Apparently so. And that being the case, why don't we leave it there? I'll make another few devices, drop one by, and you can try it for yourself."

Mason smiled and stood, reaching his hand across the table. "Thanks. I look forward to it." He shook Jackie's hand and patted Mike on the shoulder. "I haven't been the best godfather, I know. But you just might turn out to be the best godson, bringing me an opportunity like this."

Mike beamed, pulled back his shoulders and puffed out his chest. The shiftiness dropped from his bearing and his face glowed.

23

"What do you want to do now?" Zach had been waiting in the car, listening to his iPod, while the meeting went on.

Jackie grinned. "Go back and make some more stock. You up for it?"

"Sure. No classes till tomorrow. It went well?"

"Yeah, it went well." She tapped on the steering wheel, a complex, syncopated rhythm, as she waited for a gap in traffic. Zach put his hand out, tucking her hair behind her ear, recalling her attention. She turned and smiled at him. "I hadn't realised how much I was doing everything on my own. Now with someone to help me, my dreams just got exponentially bigger."

"That's great, Jackie, that's great."

She frowned. "But what?"

"But nothing. What do you mean?"

"I heard a 'but' in your voice."

"It's nothing. Just, I kind of hoped we might go out tonight. Do something together. Like a date."

"Oh, well, sure. We can do that. Get some work done, let Bob and Sandra know I won't be there for dinner. Where do you want to go?"

"Dinner, maybe, dinner sounds good. But before that, I'd like you to take you home; I'd like you to meet my gran."

They stood outside an old, rundown state house, in the broken-down part of Ferry Road. Jackie looked up at the house with a frown. "You live here?"

"Gran won't move. She's lived here since she was born. And by the way, call her by her name, Carlotta – that's what she prefers."

Jackie gave no sign of having heard this. Her face was dark, her eyes narrow. "It's ..."

"I know. I'd love to have some money to do it up for her, some day ..."

Jackie pulled back. "Zach, there's something you haven't told me. What is it?"

He turned to her, the nervousness he had been trying to hide showing clearly now on his face. "Okay. Gran's a bit nuts. She thinks there are ghosts, here, in the house."

"And are there?"

"Don't be stupid."

"Okay. So that's a no?"

Zach put a hand to his face. His jaw came forward. He looked close to tears. "Maybe we should go. It's too ... I don't usually bring anyone home."

Jackie's face softened.

He turned to look back down the path, then back again. "It was just what you said, about acceptance. I thought you might ..."

Jackie took his hand. "It's okay. You were right. Let's go inside."

"Okay." Zach pulled her forward and opened the door. "Gran? It's me."

"I know who it is," a shaky voice called out. "And I know who you've brought with you. What were you doing lingering and muttering on the path. Don't you know it's rude to keep a lady waiting? You've taken your time."

They stepped into the main room, vibrant orange curtains drawn, making a sickly burnt light which didn't reach the corners. An old woman sat hunched in a chair. Just above her shoulder a yellow budgie swung from a perch, looking comically small after the strong bulk of Anna.

"So you're the locus."

"I'm Jackie."

"You're the centre he's been revolving around for more than a year."

Jackie looked over her shoulder at Zach. He avoided her eye.

"I couldn't bring her sooner, Gran. I wasn't sure."

"Sure of yourself or sure of her?"

"Of her." He looked at the ground. Jackie wasn't listening.

"It's very busy in here," Jackie said.

"That's my brothers and sisters. Twelve of us were brought up here, and they all returned when they passed over. I'm the last one visible."

Jackie crouched down beside her. "That must be sad for you."

"Why sad, when I feel them all around me?"

"Well, then, it sounds like a full-time job, caring for eleven other souls. Demanding."

"I manage, I manage. Someone has to."

"You don't think they could fend for themselves?"

Zach stared from one to the other. "Jackie!" he whispered in alarm. "What the hell are you talking about? You sound as mad as her!"

"Language!" Carlotta admonished. "You've never called me mad before."

"No-one's ever agreed with you before. Don't encourage her," he whispered to Jackie. "I humour her, but don't tell her she's right."

Jackie gazed at the old woman. "Zach, be calm. Why did you want me here?"

"This is ... this is where I live. Gran raised me. I live here still, while I'm a student ..."

"Don't talk as if you'd leave me. How would you fend for yourself?"

"Gran!"

"I'm embarrassing you, am I? You can't hide anything from this one. She sees. She knows. And she won't judge you. She'd never judge. You or anyone."

"You got that right." Zach grumbled. "She's got no taste, sometimes."

The old woman laughed. "Condemned out of his own mouth."

"I didn't mean ..." Confusion was growing into anger. Jackie put her hand out, cautionary, and continued to look around.

"But you're not his grandmother."

"No, that's right. Great-grandmother. The only one left. The others, all the others, the family, are wanderers. But they'll come back here, in the end. It may be too late for me to see it. But Zachie's got to keep the old house sweet, for the time they do come, and pass it on, pass it on, and keep the light of sympathy going."

Jackie was silent for a long time, shifting, considering what to say. She pulled up a chair and sat near the old woman.

"He may not want that. He may want to come with me, now, for his own wandering soul."

"How would he afford it? I don't fear."

"I don't want you to fear, old woman. But accept. Respect. He's not your slave."

Zach's face was scared now. The old woman was rising from her chair in anger. "How dare you speak these words to me?"

Again Jackie sat silent. Finally she spoke to herself aloud. "I didn't expect this."

"I said how dare you?" Carlotta rose as she spoke.

"Sit down, old woman. You can't dominate me. Co-operation is my way. And we need to co-operate, if we are to find a way."

"A way to what? Come on, Jackie, let's go. Gran, I'll be back later."

Jackie turned to him, shoulders flexing as if she were warding off enemies behind her back. "Don't you see, Zach? It's better if you come with me. You're not ... considered ... here."

"He belongs to me. You can't touch him."

"You knew I was coming, old lady. I am not your enemy. If you will allow me to help you, call me back, but you won't hold his soul any more, without his choosing."

"You won't tell him!" Carlotta shrieked, her face like molten stone.

"Yes," Jackie said, her voice barely audible over the old woman's breathing. "I will."

She stood and stepped back towards the door, Zach's hand in hers. He pulled against her, feebly, for one brief instant, then allowed her to pull him from the room.

She walked firmly down the path, Zach stumbling behind. "She said ... she said I was to bring you. She said she'd make you welcome. Why were you so cruel to her? You made her angry. She'll follow."

"No, Zach. She can't follow. But come. It would be cruel to stay here. Let us leave her to grieve."

"Grieve! Grieve! What do you mean? I've got to go back."

"Zach! Do you trust me?"

"I don't understand!"

"Do you trust me?"

" ... Yes ..."

"Then get in the car. I'll explain."

24

"Jackie ..."

"Just wait. I'm thinking where to go."

"You have to answer my questions."

"I will. Give me a moment to think. Yes. That's it." They pulled in to the side of the road near the Arts Centre and strolled in through a stone arch to a wide courtyard, bordered partially by a colonnade. "We need somewhere safe, and old." She sat on a park bench, under the arches, looking out towards a grass lawn, and further off, a pond. "I should have guessed it. I knew there was something."

"What?"

"How old are you, Zach?"

"Twenty-three. You know that."

Jackie pressed her lips together and did not contradict him. "And you've always been shy. A little scared of people. But you trusted me, right from the start."

"You're nice. Pretty. Sexy."

She smiled, folding this away for later. "But you don't trust everyone else."

"I don't trust anyone else."

"What's it been like for you, with your gran?"

"She's been good to me, looked after me."

"And home. Was it peaceful?"

He frowned, as if he didn't understand the question.

"I mean, aside from the pretty thing, did you feel anything the same at home as you feel around me? Were you okay going home after school, for example?"

"Well ... sometimes I'd stay out, till I got hungry. But don't make her out a monster. She needs me. That's why she liked to keep me at home."

"And that thing she said about you staying in the house, after she dies?"

"She's always said that. You know what people are like, wanting their things to be their immortality."

"Things, or souls? Zach, I understand what she's doing, but it's wrong."

"What's she doing?"

"She's made herself a museum, for every lost soul she's ever known. You're her only link to the living, but she has to let go. She has to let those people go."

"You're saying there are ghosts there? Jackie? In the house?"

"Not in the house. She's packed them into her tiny body, she's bursting with them."

"Real people?"

"No Zach, of course not. Their memories. She's eating herself alive fuelling their memories. She needs to be able to let them go. Not try to pass them on, to you."

Zach stared straight ahead. "But ... how ... I don't even know them, most of them."

"And she hasn't told you stories?"

"Oh, so many stories, one after another, meaningless, mindless stories, all the time." He sighed it out, an anguished sigh, as if it were a great relief, finally, after years of holding it in.

"She needs to let them go. For both of you."

"But how? How can she do that?"

"Someone will have to help her."

"But who? I don't know how."

"No. I know. It will have to be me."

Jackie stood on the path again, alone, now in the full light of bright day. Zach was at college, mind only half on his work, she knew.

"Carlotta!"

"Come back, are you? Come back for forgiveness?"

"Yes. I have."

The old woman chuckled in triumph.

"I've come back to forgive you."

A loud humph followed this qualification. "Forgive me? Trollop. Seducing my boy. Breaking my faith. Attacking my life. Forgive me?"

"Freely."

"Silence. I do not accept. I do not accept the need for it."

"Then why, old woman? Why the need to keep these souls? Why not let them go?"

"How? How do you see them?"

"I see them in you. I see so much strain you are about to burst. You can just let go. They're all right. You can let them go."

"But if I let them go, they're nothing. I've failed them. Again."

"They are not your responsibility. You have tired yourself, exhausted yourself. Time for your life. Time for your needs and desires."

"No. It can't be true."

Jackie squatted down beside her chair. She held out her hand and took the other woman's in her own. The bird fluttered down and rested on Jackie's shoulder. The old woman started, fidgeted, wriggled, then quieted. "Rest now. Rest. Let go."

A long pause followed, a sense of ebbing. She thought the old woman had fallen asleep. There was a jerk, a violent twitch, and she came awake again, spluttering. "But no! No! I can't! It can't be true."

"You know it is true, Carlotta. You know it. Why deny?"

"Because if it is ... if it is ... I've wasted my life."

"No. There has been love. Laughter. Talk."

"Not since they left, not since they went. There was the boy, but he was so small, when he came to me, only a baby, no power of speech. So I told him stories. Ah, it was such a relief, to tell him the stories. They came alive again. It was company again. And they were so real."

Jackie mused, silent. She squeezed the old woman's hand once more and stood up. "All right. All right. I see. Have peace, old woman. Tell your stories." She took the bird from her shoulder and placed it on Carlotta's arm. "I'll be back, in a couple of days."

Possible solutions played in her mind as she drove towards Bob's house, rounding the city in a creative arc, finding the unfamiliar route by instinct. There was probably more than one way to give the old lady peace.

25

Jackie looked at her wrist. She had planned to get Mason's Mood Meter made and delivered this afternoon, and time was running short. She sighed, took a slow breath in and held it. Getting wound up wouldn't help. On impulse she indicated in and pulled off the road, shutting off the engine and stretching out her hands to the top of the steering wheel, closing her eyes. She played an image of greeting Mason cheerfully, handing over a Mood Meter, hearing his excited update on progress. This was what she had expected today would bring, not this complication with Carlotta. Breathe again. Trust. This would work out for the best, too.

She returned to the image of the optimistic scene with Mason. Slowly her breathing calmed, her pulse rate dropped. Within a minute her Mood Meter gave its two-tone signal: alpha state. Good. She turned to the device with a beatific smile. She didn't need to make another. She had this one.

As she pulled back onto the road, she altered course, and fifteen minutes later arrived in the car park of Mason's office.

"Here. You said you'd like one to try. Do you have time for me to tell you how it works?"

"Sure, yes, I'm fascinated."

"Then let me just get my laptop."

Mason watched the screen as Jackie displayed the various patterns. He nodded intently as she pointed out the signature profiles. "This is anger, this is fear."

"They look the same ... how can you tell?"

"Here, the sweat profile. They both produce a rise in pulse rate, but fear usually comes with a greater increase in sweat. At the moment it's all anecdotal – I'm asking people to record the emotion so I can identify the profile."

"And you'd like me to do that as well?"

"If you're willing, it'd be great." She watched for his reaction, then pulled out a notebook and described how to record the relevant information.

"And tell me again how people use it?"

"That's still revealing itself. There are several applications. Mood control is the general term. For people who want to manage anger, this alerts them they are getting into a dangerous state before they would be consciously aware – hopefully in time to take a different course. For trauma, the same thing: people don't realise what is happening when trauma memories are triggered. They disappear from the present and re-experience the trauma as if it is happening now – the Mood Meter can alert them and bring them back." Jackie nodded to herself. "That's the negative side. On the positive, I use it to generate a state of flow – alpha and theta brain waves rather than busy beta. It helps me get perspective, work from the bigger view rather than getting caught in the detail. There are two alerts – the negative mood, to shake you out of it, and the positive, a soft, two-tone bleeping that allows you to stay in the positive state."

She turned from the screen to face him, reading incomplete comprehension. "Just try it. Like Mike said. It will become clear. And once it is, I know you'll see the same potential in it that I do – it's simple and potentially life changing. That and it's much smaller than the tents, logistically a piece of cake. For me, I think this is the one, the Holy Grail, my life's work."

"But the tents are pretty good, too. I had my assistant research camping shows. How do you feel about being in Auckland the week after next? There's a big expo, I've booked us a stand."

"So soon?"

"But you can be ready, right? It's just one set-up, and we'll take orders."

"Sure. Fine." Jackie's mind flicked around her other responsibilities. "I'm sure it will work out."

Jackie sat at Sandra's dining table watching her peel potatoes. The efficiency of the movement was mesmerising, and Jackie absently rubbed her wrist, missing the soft bleeping that would normally be triggered by this mood. She needed to make more devices, but not yet, not yet.

Sandra had been speaking, talking about her day. The words washed over Jackie in a soothing lull, her mind drifting on the occasional word or idea that broke through and altered the course of her thoughts. The sounding of the mood alert surprised her, caused her to jump in her chair.

"Sandra! What is it?"

She looked up to see her sister-in-law leaning against the bench, both hands gripping the edge, knuckles white. She wound back the conversation, hearing the echo of a quite innocuous description of the costumes for the end of year play.

"I still don't … what if I'm not there? It's okay, just give me a minute. Only two weeks to go, and it will all be over. I hope."

"You're still getting this? These episodes?"

Sandra turned to face her, her cheeks white. There was guilt in her eyes. "Not so often. Really. I can keep a lid on it most of the time. And it's great, it's really great, to have the alarm let me know. Before, I'd realise I'd been catatonic for twenty minutes, half an hour, caught up in terror. Maybe if I had a project, something to do. I'll make the costumes, but that doesn't occupy my mind. I need something to take me out of myself. Just two weeks. Only two more weeks."

"God, I hate this."

"I know. I'm glad you're here, though. I just have to keep it brave for Bob. The look on his face if he thinks I'm unhappy …"

"Something to take you out of yourself …"

"Yeah. Any ideas? It would have to be somewhere I could take Clara."

"I think I have the perfect thing."

"What?"

"Let me think it through. I need to go out now, get some work done. You'll be okay?"

"Sure. Dinner in half an hour."

26

Jackie had just finished the four Mood Meters she had parts for when Zach turned up in the doorway to the workshop, a sad, remorseful expression on his face.

"I'm sorry, really sorry."

She took his hand and led him to a chair. "Why? For what?"

"For yelling at you. For not thanking you for trying to help."

"It's okay, really it is. You've lived with this your whole life. I get it. I'm glad to understand the things I couldn't make sense of."

"I feel bad about Gran, too. I should have seen ..."

"We don't see what creeps up on us. You both need help. I think I've got the answer, or the beginning of it. And I think it could be an answer for many others, too."

He stared at the ground, no evidence of the spark of hope Jackie had expected.

"You don't want to hear my idea?" She was teasing, gently, suppressing her disappointment.

He shrugged. "Okay."

"Your gran needs another place to hold her stories. Somewhere that will live on after she is gone."

"You mean me."

"No, that's just it. I thought of recordings, interviews. I was going to do it, but ... " She frowned. "I hate saying it, because it feels like giving in to the modern malaise, thinking doing is more important than being there for people. But I really don't have time at the moment. And my focus is elsewhere. This is an important time for my ... wow, I guess I have to call it a career now." A complex mixture of emotion surged through her: pride, excitement and distraction.

"It's okay. If someone needs to help her ... she's my responsibility." His shoulders slumped even further.

"It's not about responsibility, it's about everybody getting what they need. I need to focus on my work. You need a break from being her only lifeline. She needs to let go, pour out the fullness of her heart before it bursts, and Sandra needs a distraction, something positive to do for someone else. It's a perfect circle. Synergy."

Zach tilted his head, looking up at her sideways through his fringe. His lips pressed forward in a despondent pout.

She stepped over and put an arm around him. "You'll be fine, really."

They pulled apart as his wrist started the two-tone bleeping of the alpha state. "That's odd." Jackie said. She peered at the readout. "How do you feel? This doesn't feel like alpha state."

"I think I'm depressed. I think I'm very, very depressed. And maybe getting sick."

Jackie put a hand on his forehead. "You're very hot."

"I don't want to go home."

"I know." She cast around. "Maybe Sandra would let me pitch a tent in her back yard. You could stay there."

"Not a hammock, please! And don't leave me alone."

"Okay, okay." The stress in his voice alarmed her. "Hold still. Wait here."

She went inside, appearing later looking a little relieved. "Yes, I'll do the tent. We can borrow the spare bed from the boys' room. I'll stay in the hammock, beside you, so you can call if you need anything."

Half an hour later it was all set up and Zach was installed in the bed, a cold compress on his forehead, a glass of water within reach. He had taken some Paracetamol and was relatively calm. As he drifted off to sleep, Jackie slipped off his Mood Meter and plugged it into her computer. She frowned as she identified the moment of low pulse. It looked like alpha state. This wasn't good, it was too big a mistake to make. A moment later, however, her expression cleared. There. The sweat. Alpha state didn't produce sweat, but this low state, maybe indicating illness, did.

She sat back, temporarily satisfied, but still wondering. What about depression separate from illness? How would she identify that? Her nose wrinkled. This thing was further from being commercially ready than she had hoped.

She left him sleeping and slipped back into the workshop. Maybe here she could find herself again. Her eyebrow peaked as a stream of faces ran in front of her mind's eye, attended by unfamiliar feelings. She wasn't used to having people see her as their saviour.

Four o'clock saw her still up, still rhythmically sewing, assembling, packing. Ten chairs, four hammocks and two tents lay stacked in a heap to one side of the workbench. Idly she noted that she was working faster than ever. It felt like life had speeded up, her own purpose had come into focus. If only she could follow it without distraction.

She sat down and ran a hand over one eye. Of course she was happy to support Sandra and Bob. They'd been so good to her, so kind, over so many years. Of course Zach couldn't help being sick, although this wasn't what her vague images of a relationship had been like. It wasn't Craig's fault that her circumstances had changed. He wasn't asking her to feel guilty about the delay to their joint plans. Mike was only a theoretical distraction, requiring no input, like a mosquito on an island holiday. And Mason – wasn't he putting in more energy than he was taking out? It wasn't his fault there was work to do to satisfy the progress he was creating. And Carlotta? Well, she couldn't help it. Jackie closed her eyes, reached for the light switch and found her way by instinct to her tent, to her hammock, and to long-delayed sleep.

27

"You'll be okay here on your own? I'll only be a couple of hours. I just need to train the student Bob has starting. I'll feel better once I know the marketing calls I promised to make for him are being handled ... Really, Zach? You'll be fine?"

He looked up at her. His face was still flushed but he had been reaching for his glass of water on his own, and had eaten some toast for breakfast. "Of course. You go. I'm sorry to be so pathetic."

Jackie frowned and scratched her head. What was that, that thing she saw? Something was changing other than him getting better. "Sandra's with your gran today ..."

"I know. You told me. Thanks."

She shook her head. "I'm not asking for gratitude ... I just ... something's happening."

He tilted his head to one side. "Why are you looking at me like that?"

As he asked the question, her face broke into a wide smile. "Something good's happening."

"What?"

She just shrugged, still smiling. "You'll be okay."

"I already told you that. You know you can be infuriating sometimes." But she didn't hear him. She kissed him on the forehead and stepped to the exit, lingering for another brief moment before letting the tent flap fall behind her.

She opened the door of Bob's office to find him demonstrating the computer system to a girl in thigh-length boots, mini-skirt and low-cut top. "Hey, Sis. This is Janine."

"Hi Janine."

"I was just showing her how to get this thing to work."

Jackie raised an eyebrow. "I think she probably knows how a mouse works, don't you, Janine?"

"Yeah. Sure."

Bob took a step back, his eyes tracking involuntarily down the girl's body as she turned in the swivel chair, legs crossed, to face them.

"You okay, Bob? You seem distracted." He said nothing, just cleared his throat. "Anyway, I'm happy to train her. I'll show her the files, the list, and we'll go through a few calls. Easy. You can get back to work if you like. I'll only be here half an hour."

It seemed to take an effort, but Bob slunk back to his own desk and picked up some paper. Jackie got Janine to bring up the Excel document with her notes and opened the drawer to take out the file she had collected. Neither of them turned as Bob excused himself to go out and check on the manufacturing.

'One thing down.' Jackie thought with relief as she drove back to check on Zach. She reached the house at the same time as Sandra and gave way for her to drive in first.

"How was it?"

Sandra's face was glowing. "Wow. It was amazing. Such amazing stories. It should be a movie."

"Not too harrowing?"

"No. Not at all. There were unpleasant bits, as there are in all lives, but love, so much love. Incredible."

Jackie nodded. "I see." Her face reflected mild surprise. "I'm glad. You recorded it?" Sandra held up the small device and nodded. "And you're going back?"

"Tomorrow." Sandra turned to open the back door of the car and lifted Clara out of her car seat. "And she loved this one. They hit it off in a second. I've never seen Clara so quiet. She was playing with her toys, but then once Carlotta got into full song she just sat with her mouth open and listened."

"Full what?"

"Full swing. Into the story."

"That isn't what you said. You said full song."

"Did I? Funny. Actually that's more what it was. It was more like music than words. Like an instrument fuelled by emotion. You know what I mean?"

Jackie stared at her lovely but usually prosaic sister-in-law. "Yes. I do. I know exactly." Sandra continued speaking, but Jackie's listening rolled on the sounds like she was body-surfing. A minute later she turned with no farewell and walked around the house to the tent to find Zach.

"You okay? I could feel you calling."

"I heard your voice. I was waiting to see you. Yeah. I'm okay. Much better. I could go home now, if you want. You don't want to be looking after me forever."

"Yes, I do, actually. I don't want you to go. But if you're up to it, get dressed, I could use some help."

28

Jackie watched as Zach assembled the third Mood Meter. Her tongue played around her top lip as she willed him to get a small component into place. He wasn't as fast as she was, or as deft, but it would be great if he could learn to do this – it would free her up and mean he might accept the money she wanted to offer him without his pride refusing it. It was nearly the end of the college year, he would need a summer job and she wanted him close. Her mobile rang and she took it outside to answer it so he wouldn't be distracted at this critical moment.

"Hello?" The greeting was cautious. Hardly anyone phoned her.

"It's Mason. Can you come in again? There's someone I'd like you to meet."

"Sure. Now?"

"If you can."

"And ..?"

She heard muffled speech, and a crackling, as if he had put his hand over the microphone. Then he came back clear.

"It's probably easiest to explain once you get here."

"And the person you want me to meet is in the room with you, so you don't want to talk in detail."

"That's right."

"Sure. See you in ten."

She opened the workshop door again. Zach's tongue was out as he finally clicked the little piece into place. She waited a second, watching the satisfied look on his face, smiling to herself. He looked over at her.

"Hey there. Good work."

"Thanks."

"Listen, I have to go out for a while. Would you mind keeping going? We could use a few more of those. I'll get the rest of the cases while I'm out."

"Okay. Sure."

She turned to go, then on impulse turned back and pocketed the three devices he had completed. Then she hesitated a moment longer and looked into his eyes, leaning sideways to kiss him. The moment was long, suspended. Slowly her eyes opened, she pulled back a fraction, breaking contact, then moved quietly towards the workshop door. It swung quietly closed behind her. She was gone before Zach opened his eyes.

She felt buoyant, moving uncharacteristically fast, observing the change of pace with interest as she breezed past Mason's assistant and pushed open his door.

"Hi. Jackie." Mason held out his hand to shake hers. She adapted to the formality without betraying her surprise.

"Mason." She gave a short nod and turned to his guest: a slim woman, stylishly dressed, about his own age, leaning back with false relaxation on the sofa in the corner of the office. Words flashed through Jackie's mind.

'She fancies him. And she's pretending that she doesn't. And it's none of my business.'

Jackie held out her hand. "Jackie, this is Dr Catlins. Jackie Fromm."

The woman shook Jackie's hand reluctantly, looked her dismissively up and down, then turned her intense attention back to Mason. 'And Mason has no clue.'

"I was telling Dr Catlins about your invention, the Mood Meter. I thought she might be willing to set up a clinical trial of it, help us get more usable information."

The woman broke in. "And I was explaining that that might not be as easy as it sounds. You have very crude information here, it's likely that any usefulness would be drowned in the noise of statistical uncertainty."

"Still, Pandora. We said we'd try."

"Of course we'll try."

"Well then. I haven't explained it well, I'll get Jackie to do it properly. Then perhaps you can set up another time to meet, to get things underway."

"The three of us to meet?"

"No. You don't need me. Totally ignorant."

"In this one area perhaps ..." Pandora gave an ingratiating smile from which Mason recoiled.

"In general. Totally ignorant." He laughed unconvincingly and backed away a step. "Jackie. Go ahead. Did you bring your laptop? I should have said."

"I have it. And here are three more of the Mood Meters. You have the basic concept? Of measuring pulse and sweat and using a diary."

Pandora inclined her head, eyes flicking occasionally to Mason, who stared studiously at Jackie's face.

"So let me show you some of the data we've collected so far ..."

29

Pandora's face reflected more and more interest as Jackie went through the graphs, indicating trends and patterns and outlining her theories. She was nodding and staring intently at the screen.

They both jumped, heads banging together, as Pandora's phone alarm went off. She took the phone out of her pocket and read the reminder.

"I have a meeting. But there's definitely a lot to talk about. Why don't you email me and we'll set up a time to look into this in more detail. I have a couple of under-employed graduate students at the moment ... this could be just the thing."

Jackie's eyes stayed on the door a moment after it closed behind Pandora.

"How do you two know each other?" she asked, when she could feel Mason getting uncomfortable with the silence. She turned as she spoke, and watched his face as he answered.

"We were at school together. She was the brains, I was the bad influence."

"And you were never ..."

"What? Oh! God no! She's far too clever for me. Besides, she went away, to university, and I'd left school anyway. Started working here, as a delivery boy. No qualifications, nothing. She'd never go for anyone like me."

"There is more than one type of intelligence. You know that. I think you should ask her."

"What? No! No." There was a moment's silence, then. "Actually I was thinking of asking you."

Jackie's already still posture froze into immobility. There was a beat, two, where it would have been better if she had spoken. She gave a tiny shake of the head. "That wouldn't work. That wouldn't work at all."

Jackie left Mason's office in a state of ambivalence. One more complication, but also a huge opportunity. She didn't have the resources or the training to turn the Mood Meter into a widely marketable item. Pandora was exactly who she needed.

She stopped short of her car, incapable of turning the key, unlocking the door and getting in. Instead, her feet led her on through the car park to where a path ran along the river towards the city's most popular bars. The Strip. She never came here. So why now?

None of the bars called to her, and she crossed Hereford Street at the traffic lights and turned right. On the left was an independent bookshop. Scorpio. She didn't come here often, but it drew her now.

Towards the back of the shop was a red leather swivel chair, pulled up to a table of assorted coffee table books. She sat down, lodging her feet on the wheel struts and twisting her hips so the seat turned back and forth. Idly, she reached out and turned a book over. There was a cartoon on the back, a naked man holding a strategically placed pot-plant. The caption read

"Sage advice." Jackie frowned. For a moment it didn't make sense. Her eyes flicked around the image. In the background was a woman sitting up in bed, hair in curlers, teeth in a jar on the bedside table, leering at him. Jackie twitched in frustration. Then she noticed text running around the side of the pot. "Whether you think you can, or think you can't, you're probably right." She turned the book over again and looked at the front cover. *The Little Green Book of Garden Humour*. Garden humour. Sage, a pot of sage. Of course. Gardeners always saw things a little quirkily. Now she started laughing out loud.

Thinking of Craig, and wanting a peace offering when she turned up there again having been away so long, she took the book to the counter. Part way through the transaction, however, she asked the assistant to wait and followed a second, stronger pull into the corner section, children's books. She felt odd, like there was something she was missing, but she didn't know what.

Following the same instinct, she found a second book in her hands: *Grandad's Gone to Heaven*. She opened it and discovered it was one of those preachy books, in this case trying to get children to accept the idea of death. There were others around that struck her as similar, claiming to be entertaining stories, but really moralistic tales about using the toilet properly, or being polite to people. This idea disturbed Jackie. Children should be allowed to use their judgement, be rude if that was what their intuition told them to do. How could you tell them not to get in the car with a stranger if they have no choice about kissing Auntie Muriel on the cheek?

Her thoughts strayed, her face reflecting uncharacteristic distress. Finally she looked back at the book in her hands and almost dropped it. She placed it on the table and turned away, but something pulled her back. Reluctantly she added it to her purchase and took out her wallet again to pay.

"Actually, can you gift wrap that one for me?" She didn't want Sandra to see it, she'd think Jackie had lost all hope, all compassion.

30

It was a relief to get to the market on Saturday, a place she knew, where every movement was easy, every transaction complete and done. Zach was in his place, within breathing distance, but occupied, too. She could let her thoughts be her own.

There was a change of tempo. She noticed it by about halfway through the morning. It was subtle, but distinct. The conversations she was having were more purposeful, people seemed to want something different from normal from her. Most weeks they wandered vaguely, talked idly, dithered and came back to buy or didn't. Today they were decisive, nodding more sharply. "That looks excellent. We'll take it. In fact, we'll take six."

The day came to an end and she was counting wads and wads of cash. No credit cards today, just people making trips to the cash machine or pulling stacks of the stuff from their wallets. She considered banking it before she headed home, but as she was turning towards the other side of the market area where the machine was, her mobile beeped. Sandra. She was attempting text language, but had it combined with predictive text, so it took a while to work out the meaning.

"Zach!"

He stuck his head around the edge of the stall. "Yeah?"

"Are you almost ready? Sandra wants me to come to Carlotta's. She says she needs help."

Zach looked at his stall, and hers, still standing. "Do you think it's urgent?"

"I don't know. Maybe."

"You'd better go. I'll take these down and join you."

At the look on Zach's face, Jackie set off running. He knew what Carlotta was capable of, far more than she.

At the curb she paused. Everything looked calm and quiet. Jackie felt no urgency as she walked up the path. She even took out her cell phone to read the text that arrived as she was approaching the door. Sandra again. "False alarm. All okay now."

At that moment she heard a burst of familiar laughter, two people, then three, then four, chiming and clashing together in raucous hysterics. She pushed back the door without knocking. Clara ran to her, pelting full tilt on legs that were unused to taking full responsibility for the body above them.

Through on the sofa, Carlotta was heaving with mirth, the air was a blur of green, red and yellow feathers, and there was Craig, in between bouts of hysterics, mimicking a sports commentator, using a carrot as a microphone. "And the parrot laps the budgie for the twenty-fourth time. I think we have what we in Cornwall call a clear victory! Victory to the parrot!"

"Craig! How did you get here? And Sandra? All this time I thought you were sane."

Sandra turned to her with tears of laughter streaming down her face. Clara's high, delighted chuckle fluttered into the micro-silences left by the three adults. Sandra pulled Clara off Jackie's leg, scraping ineffectively at her own face with her denim sleeve, making no progress towards drying it. Jackie's face relaxed, her eyes softening. "It is good to see you smiling. It really is."

On pretence of making a cup of tea, Jackie lead Sandra out. "Where did he come from? How is he here?"

"He turned up at home. Gave me a bit of a fright, to be honest. Said he was looking for you."

"Well, I get that, but how did he know how to find me? You?"

"That was even more worrying. He said he went through your things, in the tent you left behind. Who is he, anyway?"

"Campground owner."

"And he followed you, why?"

Jackie shrugged.

"What is it about you, that men can't seem to resist you?"

"They resist me. What are you talking about?"

"I mean they fancy you. All of them. Thank God you're Bob's sister, or I couldn't stand the sight of you."

"It's not all of them!" But she scanned through her acquaintance and frowned. There did seem to have been a lot of propositions lately. "Anyway, I'm with Zach now, I told you."

"Well, did you tell Craig?"

Jackie looked back at Craig doubtfully. “Didn’t realise it was necessary, actually.” She scratched her head and closed her eyes. “I have a feeling this is going to be complicated.”

They both watched him for a few seconds, going through a photograph album that Carlotta held on her lap, until they both looked up, catching the two women staring. Guiltily Jackie and Sandra turned back to the teapot. “Found any teabags?”

“Yes, here.” Their voices were exaggerated and unconvincing, but the tea was made and they went back into the lounge to serve it. Seconds later the door banged open and Zach stood panting in the doorway.

31

Zach's hands tensed at his sides, ready to take necessary action, whatever that might be. The demands of holding a teacup and making polite conversation were both too little and too much for him; pumping adrenaline caused the cup to shake and clatter on its saucer.

"What's going on?" he whispered, when the conversation around the album rose to allow him to speak unheard.

"I'm not sure, but I'm dealing with it."

Zach frowned as he watched Craig look into his great-grandmother's eyes and smile. Craig's eyes flicked to Jackie and back to the old woman with a look of triumph and joy. Jackie flinched, then tried to hide it, then began to laugh.

Sandra gave her a questioning look.

"I think at least one of my problems is solved," Jackie whispered, so only Sandra could hear. "Maybe more than one. And Zach's, too. Who'd have thought it? I never would have thought of it, it's too good to be true. Hey Craig!" She lifted her voice to be heard by the room in general. "I brought you a present." She moved to stand, but Clara on her knee protested. Jackie turned to Zach. "Would you get it? A book. In the back of my car. In a Scorpio bag."

Zach looked relieved to make an exit. He left shaking his head, muttering. "This is all too bizarre." Within a minute he returned with the bag, reaching inside it and pulling out, not the innocuous garden humour but the time-bomb gift-wrapped package. Before Jackie could stop him, Craig had ripped it open. His eyes reflected confusion, then pain.

"Is this a joke? You making a joke? You implying I can't read?"

"No! No! Not that, this." She leaned forward to rectify it, handing him the other book, not noticing Clara reach down and pick up the one he dropped by his side as he took it.

Clara uttered her first ever two-word sentence: "Mummy, story," and Jackie turned in slow motion, her face a silent scream.

Back in the tent in Sandra's back yard, Jackie sat across from Sandra and watched her take a steadying breath. Her hand was wrapped around a now-cold mug of tea. A pile of tissues spilled across the metal table, one or two tumbled onto the floor. The tissue box was empty, and Sandra held the last one, screwed up and smeared with tears, in her left hand.

"I'm so, so sorry. I still don't know why. It was just there, in my hand, demanding to be bought. You know I don't over-think things. I just bought it. But I never meant you to see it, not now, not like that."

Sandra reached across and patted Jackie's hand. "You keep repeating yourself. It's all right. Really it is. I needed a really good cry, and I hadn't had one."

"But you were fine. You seemed fine."

"Did you really think that? I was just holding together. Suppressing the fear. It wasn't going to last forever."

"But the Mood Meter – you said it helped."

"It did. It took away the abject absent terror of it. That wasn't helping me, letting the fear take over. But this, letting the grief out; this I needed to do. See the difference?"

"Yes and no. I hate being the cause. But I can see you're calmer now."

"Calmer than I've been in a fortnight. And you weren't the cause. You just made a crack in the dam." She smiled, with a small exhale that was a microcosmic laugh. "And you were there with the bucket to bail out the flood of tears. Bob would have freaked out if I had come inside like this. Don't beat yourself up. Really. I needed it."

"Now who's repeating herself?" Jackie took a deep breath in. "Are you ready for bed? I have to be on the plane to Auckland early tomorrow, for the trade show."

"But it's Saturday." Sandra glanced at the clock. "And it's only seven o'clock. Bob would think I was mad if I went to bed now."

"After raising me, his definition of mad is a little clearer than that. Are you saying you're not tired?"

"Now that you mention it, yeah, I am. Exhausted."

"Washed out."

"Empty."

"Drained to the dregs."

"Ready to meet the sandman."

"And out of clichés."

Sandra stood, stretching and placing the camp chair in close to the table. "Thanks for the tea."

"No problem. I'll see you before I go."

Jackie leaned her head on Zach's shoulder as he drove her to the airport. They were early, and she gripped his arm and held him still as he made to get out of the car. "Let's just sit here for a while. Maybe forever."

"Whatever you like. You know I don't want you to go."

"I know." She sighed. "So much is happening. It's all happening. I have dreamed of doing something, something more, for so long, it's hard to believe it's coming true."

"You're talking like you wanted this. You didn't, did you? You were happy, selling at the market."

"I was happy, and I wanted something more, too. It's just, I've imagined parts of it, and not taken time to think it through. I knew I wasn't doing all I could with what I have, that if I wanted to benefit the wider world, things would have to get bigger. I just didn't think through what that would mean for my life."

"Like what?"

"Like travel. Like finding you and having to leave you, even for a few days. We haven't had time to relax yet. We haven't had time to enjoy ourselves, and I'm not sure what happened. Why haven't we just sat together, like this, so much earlier than now?"

"I took you to meet Gran, remember."

Jackie smiled, a peaceful, beatific smile. "That's right. You did. So this bit isn't my fault. That's such a relief."

"It is?"

She leaned up to kiss him. He moved into it with enthusiasm, but too soon she pulled away, putting her hand to the door latch. "Okay. Time to go. Wish me luck."

32

Mason was waiting near the check-in desks. Zach scowled at him and bowed backwards out of the terminal, scarcely giving Jackie time to place her hand on his cheek in farewell.

"Boyfriend's grumpy," Mason commented, with minimal interest.

"Yes. He doesn't like you."

Mason's eyebrows raised. "Why not?"

"He's jealous."

"Did you tell him there's no need to be? You've set me straight."

"It's not just that. It's your ... confidence."

Anyone less aware would have missed Mason's split-second sneer, but Jackie tasted the residue of it in the air after it had been erased from his features. "Confidence is easy."

"For those who have it."

Mason had already lost interest in the topic of Zach. "You're confident. Unusually so." He spoke with surprise, as if he had only just noticed.

Jackie shrugged. "As you say, confidence is easy for those who have it. I think as long as you know what you want from life, confidence just falls into place. Those without it are those who are trying to please others."

He shepherded her towards a free counter and handed over their tickets. "Why do people do that?" The check-in clerk looked up, ready to answer, but Jackie was already speaking.

"Because they think they have to. Or because they're scared not to. They think they'd have to survive on their own, and they think they couldn't. But they're wrong on both counts. People who know themselves are in fierce demand. And people can survive on their own. It's actually easier than being with others."

Mason lifted Jackie's new Life-in-a-Suitcase onto the conveyor. "So you say. Have you ever been on your own?"

"Of course." She focused on him with great surprise. "Of course. What did you think? I've designed a house with a hammock, made just for one."

"But you're in fierce demand, those were your words, weren't they?" He reached out and took the boarding passes, then nodded towards the check-in clerk, who stared after them as they walked away.

"I wasn't talking specifically about me. Mason, are you angry about something?"

He mumbled, distracting her by juggling his jacket, wallet and papers.

"Mason, what?" She came to a sudden halt in the middle of the concourse. A tour group parted around her, weaving through and separating them. Mason reached his arm through the crowd and pulled her close to him. She looked up into his face, her eyes clear and questioning.

"All right." He looked off in the direction of the vaguely meandering tourists. "I've never been turned down before."

"Ah." She nodded. "Pride."

"That's not it at all!"

"I'm not the one for you, Pandora is."

"Will you let go of that? It's not happening."

"Give me one reason."

He swallowed, face twitching as if random electrical impulses were firing around it. "We're at gate 5," he said. He licked his lips and rubbed the side of his forefinger, hard, against the bottom one. "She'd eat me alive. She has no mercy. You saw, at the beginning, when she didn't like you. She is merciless."

"She's frightened. She's proud, too, she won't tell you she likes you. In case you hurt her."

"Well, then, a stalemate."

"What about confidence?"

"Hers or mine?"

"Yours. Of course. Yours."

"Come on. Didn't you hear that? They're calling our flight."

She had to run after him as he strode off in the direction of the plane. "Mason! There's plenty of time. Wait!" She caught him as he was pointing her out to the ground crew, checking boarding passes at the door of the air tunnel. "What was the rush?"

His back was unresponsive as he threaded his way along the aircraft aisle in front of her. She sat down beside him and firmly closed her mouth. After a moment she reached forward and took the in-flight magazine from the seat pocket. A minute later they were poring over an article together.

"High-tech camping, luxury style."

"They've got nothing on us," Mason laughed. "Look out, world! Here we come."

33

The first day of the show went well and they came back to the hotel with lots of orders, yet something didn't feel right to Jackie. "They just didn't get it. The philosophy of it. It's a life, not a holiday; they saw it as a once a year, weeklong dream. It's a way of life."

"You have to let people do what they want. If they want to store it away in the garage for fifty-one weeks a year, why not? You've made your money."

"God, Mason! You don't actually believe that? I don't want to get rich at the expense of keeping people trapped in boxes. I want to change lives."

"There's a saying in business. Want to hear it?"

"Don't patronise me."

"Want to hear it?"

She scratched her head, then folded her arms and stood, foot tapping.

"Sell to people who want it, not to people who need it."

"But ..."

"You can't live people's lives for them. You have to let them make their own choices."

"But ..."

"Don't you? Isn't that the basis of this philosophy you keep talking about? Personal freedom."

"Yes, but ..."

"You have to let them stay in the boxes if that's what they want to do. And they don't call them boxes, incidentally, they call them houses."

"They weren't the boxes I was talking about, Smarty-pants. I was talking about their lives."

He stepped closer to her. "Now who's being patronising?"

She lowered her head and looked upwards towards him from under thunderous eyebrows. Her lower teeth came forward. "God, okay. But it still doesn't feel right."

"What do you want instead? A hippy commune? Is that it?"

"I just hate the way people don't ..." Her lip wobbled, then the stern expression returned.

His eyes fixed on hers and he moved towards her like a fish on a line. "Jackie ... are you sure ... I just ..." He put his hands out and leaned in towards her, their faces close. She pulled away, just shifting the angle of her head so that their lips would not connect.

"Mason, we've been through this."

His hands were on her shoulders. She wasn't moving away. "It's just, something pulls me to you. It feels right, to me."

She stood still, feeling the steady beat of her heart. She felt nothing one way or the other. Nothing told her it was right, nothing told her it was wrong.

"You feel so safe to be with. So strong. So confident. And yet so ... elusive. Other women I've met, it's like their personalities are flitting around the room looking for someone to settle on. You're so self-possessed. I find it compelling."

"I'm not single."

"And if you were?"

"Then things would be different. But I still wouldn't be 'flitting'. I keep myself here." She pressed her gently closed fist against her chest and nestled it into place. "I live inside myself. I don't know how others don't."

He closed his eyes and sighed. "Well, there's nothing to be done tonight."

"I thought you said we'd make a plan for tomorrow."

"Yes, that, I just meant ... You go and sit there at the table. I'll get some paper, we'll make some notes. Then do you want to go out, or shall we order room service?"

Jackie walked to the window. The hotel was high-rise, with a busy street far below. There was a maze of buildings between here and where she could see narrow strips of the harbour peeking through.

"I don't think I can face the city again. I'm tired."

"Here then, choose something. We can work until it comes."

The food sat untouched, long cold. Jackie's face was screwed up in frustration. Mason was leaning back in his chair, eyes closed. "Okay, explain it to me one more time. Why is living in it full time different from using it for holidays?"

"It isn't, necessarily. It's what they do with the rest of their time that matters."

"So we've moved away from the life the tent offers ..."

"And the furniture, and everything ..."

"To managing their lives full time. Like a religion."

"Are you being deliberately obtuse?"

"Not deliberately, no."

"Let me start from the beginning."

"You do that. Why not."

"God, I've never been so exasperated. I didn't really know what the word meant until now."

"Well, how have you explained it to others? I'm not much dumber than most. Explain it in a way that has worked before."

"I've never tried to explain it before. Not really. It's only just hit me, the ones who have bought it, kit and all, till now, already knew. They already understood it. It didn't change anything for them, not really. Just made things a little bit easier. I want to let people out of their boxes. I see them scurrying around, like ants in a jar, thinking they're happy, when all the time, little by little, their air is running out."

Mason laughed. "They don't see it like that, the little people. They really believe they are happy."

"But they're trapped ..."

He sat up, leaned forward and grabbed both her arms in his hands. "Look at me. Listen to this logic. The definition of happiness ... is thinking you're happy. If you believe you're happy, then you are."

"But ... they must be missing something. They're not free. If they saw what I see, they couldn't live like they do."

"Okay, but wait. Calm down. Consider. If you saw what they see, you couldn't live like you do." His voice was gentle, his face kind. Jackie opened her mouth to speak, then closed it.

"Is that really true? Surely not for all of them?"

"No, not for all of them. And that's where the saying comes into play: sell to the ones who want it."

"But they're not the ones who need help."

"Back there again, are we? It's slow. Think slow. Think viral. One breaks away from life, because deep down they've always known they want to. People around them go 'Hey, I didn't know you could do that, maybe I could do that, if I wanted.' And they consider that, whether they do want it, or not. And then, with the ones who do, it spreads."

"You've thought about this. I've never met anyone before who's thought about this."

"No. I haven't. I'm thinking about it now."

"You thought of all of this now?"

He shrugged. "Isn't it obvious? It's only logic, after all."

"There!"

"What?"

"There it is! Never, after this night, ever again tell me you aren't as intelligent as anyone you can name."

Mason blinked, pulling back from her.

"Hah!" she said, triumphant. "You finally got my point."

He held up his hands. "Okay. You win this one. But I think you also got mine."

He turned and lifted the stainless steel dome off a plate, taking a chip and chewing it laboriously. He glanced over towards the street window, where the traffic had reduced to its midnight buzz. "Come on. I think we'll have to brave the city if we want to eat at all tonight."

"Okay. Only one thing I need, to be able to trust you."

"I thought it was the city you were afraid of, not me. All right, what one thing?"

"Promise you'll ask Pandora out once we get back."

"Or you could ditch that boyfriend of yours. We could be great together, a team."

"Mason ..."

"Okay. Okay. That's a no. Well, what the hell, okay, I'll do it. I'll ask her out."

"Really?"

"Absolutely. Without doubt. For sure."

34

They stood together at the stand, in that odd time after the show had started, but before the first wave of pedestrians had got to them. Mason was bouncing on his feet, impatient. Jackie brushed her hair back repeatedly, then put her hand deliberately down at her side and held it there.

"So given that the whole world isn't ready for your life changes all at once, what do you want? What would represent the next successful development for you?"

"At the show?"

"At the show, with the business, whatever."

Jackie gazed across the concourse to a stand where people were selling camp stoves and barbecues. Their hook was to offer food, and an enticing smell of bacon wafted over. "I guess, then, if you're right, and we can't hope to take over the world all at once, then I'd like the people who want this to find us."

"'This' being?"

"A way to break out of the box. I'd like the people who are ready to break out of the box to find us, to love us, and to talk about us."

Mason nodded. "Okay." He wandered to the back of the stall and picked up some paperwork. Jackie watched him, her mouth opening as if she had something more to say, but he sat down, idly flicking through the sheaf of paper without looking up. She leaned out of the stall space and looked along in the direction the crowds would come. No-one in sight. She hesitated a moment, then skipped across towards the scent of breakfast.

"Hi, I'm Jackie. Any chance you could spare one of those? They smell fantastic!"

The guy in the bright green apron smiled. "My pleasure." He handed her a bacon sandwich and watched her with satisfaction as she sank her teeth in. "You sell Lives in Suitcases?"

"Yeah. My invention. It's great, I can just pick up and go, whenever I like."

"I'll have to come and take a closer look." He nodded towards the doors. "But later. Here they come! Good luck now."

"You, too. And thanks."

As with yesterday, for the first hour Jackie enjoyed herself. The change in her after that was fast, and Mason had learned to recognise it. "Why don't you take a break, go for a walk, have something to drink? I'll be fine here for a while."

"I feel guilty leaving."

"You've got that look on your face again. You're scaring people off."

"I don't know how it happens. One minute I'm fine, I love them, and the next minute I just want to poke them in the eye."

"So go! Now!" He stepped out into the concourse with an overdone smile. Jackie swung her bag over her shoulder and began to swim against the stream towards the toilets. Five minutes in a quiet cubicle, totally alone.

Jackie strolled back into the stand fifteen minutes later, face peaceful.

"My turn now," said Mason. "Back in ten. Sell, sell, sell!"

But he was considerably more than ten minutes. Jackie had been waiting to proudly tell him about the two North Island shops she had signed up, but he brought someone else with him. Her news would have to wait.

"Jackie, this is Tim." She shook his hand, feeling the dry, welcoming warmth like a day at the beach. "He's here from London, advertising the mega show they have at Earl's Court every year. He wants us to exhibit there, but better than that, he wants to join forces. I've told him about what you do, but why don't you show him?"

Tim left, patting Jackie on the shoulder and kindly wishing her well; it was like a benediction. She was turning to comment to Mason how much she liked him when someone tapped her on the shoulder, a woman with a microphone. Behind her was a huge camera. Television news.

That night they watched her slot together. The TV company had given her half the time allocated to the Camping Show, and her passion for the lifestyle she offered came through clearly on camera. Mason opened a small bottle of Deutz from the minibar and poured out two half glasses, the bubbles sparkling off the sides and fizzing out of the top onto Jackie's hand as she took it from him.

"Here's to Alternative Lifestyle's rising star." Mason raised his glass.

"The company?"

"No, Babe. You."

35

Tim was featuring her in the show promotion, and she was the first feature article in his new *Downshift* magazine.

"I think I need to do something about my clothes, though. What do you think? I looked a bit of a scarecrow on TV."

"You're you," answered Sandra. "In this market people don't want someone over-polished."

"Still, maybe a little something. Some makeup, maybe. I looked so pale. And it's a long time since I've been shopping for clothes." She pulled the sweatshirt she was wearing away from her body. "Recognise this?"

"Well, I know, it used to be Bob's. But you've been working. You can't go into the workshop in a business suit."

"Still," Jackie persisted. "Will you help me? I don't know where to start."

Sandra held up her hands. "Not me! I know nothing about fashion. There is someone, though, a friend of a friend, an image consultant. I've met her, she's nice; she'll help you. Maybe I'll come with you, celebrate the good news about my test results."

Jackie leaned over and put her hand on Sandra's. "I'm so glad, so glad you're fine."

"All that fuss for nothing." She wiped a tear away and spoke brightly. "'Course, even though he's treating me like a princess, Bob won't like me spending the money ... maybe you can treat me. You can afford it now."

Jackie grinned. "Yeah, I know, amazing! Who'd have thought?"

"We knew," Sandra said, smugly. "Bob and I always knew you'd make it."

There was a lot to do in the months before the European show. Production needed to be professional, reliable and scalable so they could handle whatever orders came in. "You'll shoot yourself in the foot if you promise and then can't deliver." This was one of Tim's favourite expressions; he used it more than would have been thought possible, by means of ingenious twists of logic. It was the only pessimistic turn of phrase he had. Jackie and Mason smiled at each other, but the point was well made and well taken. If they had to deliver thousands of kits in the next year, they needed to be ready to manufacture them, freight them and get them to their buyers.

They had decided some innovative marketing would suit the spirit of the product, and Jackie had had a brain wave: to get Craig's lease tents up and running and make a pseudo-documentary, about life in a Kiwi campground. They'd use it at the trade stand, and with luck find a quirky angle so it would go viral on YouTube.

Tim was optimistic. "That's the ideal. And if not, we hand sell, one at a time, until the world starts talking. And it will. Get the footage taken and send it to me. Then we can brainstorm how we put it together."

In an unbelievably short time, Craig's campground was transformed. In exchange for the lease of the top row of sites for the next four summers, Mason and Jackie's new company built the kitchen block and a luxurious shower block, expanded the developed area and even brought in some ten-year-old trees to boost the look of the new land and provide shade and shelter for years to come. Craig would receive half the income from the Lifestyle Tents. He went to town and spent half the first year's income on a new titanium leg, and a pair of shorts to show it off.

"Don't hide my gold teeth, do I? And this thing's twice as valuable."

Jackie had weekly meetings with Pandora to keep up-to-date with the Mood Meter trials. They were going well, starting to form into something concrete that could be the basis of a website and materials to send to clinical psychologists. There were two main markets – the mentally unwell and the self-help junkies. Mason joked that he couldn't see the difference. Pandora, eager to please in their fledgling relationship, laughed so heartily that Jackie wanted to thump her.

"There's nothing wrong with people wanting to improve their lives," Jackie asserted.

Mason sneered. "There's a difference between self-improvement and self-delusion."

"Is there? I would never have known. If you don't believe in it, then I don't want you. You can take your money and make some other person's dreams come true."

"Now Jackie," Mason glanced at Pandora before putting his arm around Jackie's shoulders. "I didn't mean to offend."

"Fuck you. You know you're a bastard, don't you?"

"Loveable bastard, though."

"There's no such thing."

"Now you two ..." Pandora put in. "Kiss and make up."

Jackie finally succeeded in shrugging Mason off. "I don't know why you do this. You're just winding me up, and Pandora, too. You don't need to keep testing us. Why don't you just accept we both love you? Oh, for goodness' sake, Pandora, I didn't mean it like that. You're as bad as he is. Now show me those graphs again. What can we use them to say?"

36

Zach was out of college for the summer and had finally mastered sleeping in a hammock. The longer he stayed out of his gran's house, the more relaxed he became.

"But I feel guilty, leaving her there on her own. She must be lonely."

"I visit, and Sandra, and Craig, with Anna."

"Craig." Zach shook his head.

"Get to know him. He's a mystic. A visionary."

"He's creepy."

"And creepy, yeah. But in a good way."

Zach laughed, tousling Jackie's hair. "You're so weird! Who'd have thought I'd fall for you?"

"Everybody falls for me. That's just the way I am."

Zach looked at her with moon eyes. "Yeah, I know, drives me crazy."

"Zach! I didn't mean it. Can't you tell when I'm joking?"

"Not when what you say is true. And it does drive me crazy, except when I'm with you, alone, like now."

"And then it's me who drives you crazy."

"Except when you let me kiss you. So give me a break, put me out of my misery, come here."

She smiled. "I love seeing you happy."

"Then stop talking, and come here."

"I want the factory to be a great place to work: fun, lively, inspiring. Not a sweat shop."

"Sweat shops are cheaper," Mason teased.

"Only if you take a short-sighted view – yes, I know you were joking, but I want you to be serious. I want space, and light, and things to do in breaks. I want really high quality, and high productivity, and for that, people need to be focused and in flow."

"Okay. So tell me. How does it look?"

"We divide the space up like this." She stood back into the corner of the vast space, arms held out at right angles. "Instead of rows of sewing tables, we have a circle, so everyone can see what everyone else is doing, and they can talk to each other. The ones who prefer to keep internal focus can wear headphones, we'll provide iPods, with whatever they want to listen to."

"That's extra cost."

"You don't say. And I want this whole area here open, put aside for breaks. We'll get a state-of-the-art coffee machine ..."

"More cost ..."

"Because caffeine increases productivity. There'll be a ping pong table, juggling balls ..."

"Juggling balls!"

"Too expensive? Damn. Well, maybe I can provide those myself."

"Just humour me. Why juggling balls?"

"Because they improve left-brain/right-brain co-ordination, which improves sewing productivity and quality, they require intense focus, which helps distract the mind from any outside concerns, and they make people laugh, which increases breath quality and oxygen levels in the blood, as well as enhancing mood, which in turn increases ..."

"Productivity and quality, I get it."

"For the price of a set of juggling balls, $19.95, and as I said, I have a set already which we can use. I want this to be a place where workers love coming. I want people to be queuing up to work here. And I want to be proud to be part of it."

Mason nodded, his eyes falling on her face with admiration. "Okay. Okay. I get it. It's good."

The documentary was progressing. One of Zach's college mates was great with a camera and came out every day or so for an hour's filming of day-to-day events in the campground. The campers were usually delighted to be involved; there was just the challenge of keeping them natural. Jackie watched the rough cut of the first three weeks, laughing until tears rolled down her cheeks. "You've got a fabulous eye for the ridiculous."

Cane shrugged. "I try to keep it respectful, too. It depends what you want. Is this too off the wall? I know it's corporate ..."

"No, it's supposed to be a mind-bend. This is great. We want a YouTube explosion, and this might just do it."

"So I'll keep going?"

"Yeah, please."

37

"Zach, there's something I need to talk to you about."

He looked up from where he was moulding clay in the shade of a tree, saying nothing, waiting.

"When I go to England in April, I might not come back straight away."

"Yeah, I know."

"You do?"

"Sure. It figured. There will be lots more for you to do there, lots more than here. You're just not a small town girl."

"But I am! I am. I just have some things to do. It doesn't mean I don't love you."

He looked at her fondly. "I know. I know that. I know I can trust you."

"So you don't mind?" She took three small steps towards him, hesitated, then in a short bound she was on his knee, knocking his hand onto her jeans, leaving a smear of clay.

"Well, I do mind, but what if I came with you? I've always wanted to travel, but I couldn't leave my gran. I have some money saved, now, thanks to living here ..."

"Don't worry about the money. But would you, would you really? What about college?"

"I can delay my final year. I want to do this."

Jackie looked into the distance, alternative visions flickering before her eyes. "You know I need time to myself. We wouldn't be together every minute."

"That's how it is here. It's fine." He held his breath, watching her face. He relaxed when she smiled.

"Yeah, that looks great. Really great. I'm so glad." She kissed him on the cheek, and he held her tighter as she made to get up.

He stretched around to kiss her on the lips, pulling her into a different type of embrace, then stood, lifting her with him. He took the few steps towards the tent, and they disappeared inside, but not before a neighbour above had seen them and let out a wolf-whistle.

"Here," Zach whispered. "I think we should celebrate. It's a new level of commitment. Are you ready for it? Are you sure?"

"Yes." She watched as he unhooked the hammocks, placing them side by side on the floor, the thick down providing a mattress.

"Well, then. Come here." He wrapped his arms around her and kissed her again.

Later that night they took the hammocks outside and unrolled them under the stars. They lay side by side, gazing upwards.

"Life is strange, don't you think?"

"Strange and wonderful."

"There is so much out there, and yet, in a sense it all seems to come from in here." Jackie pointed at her chest, her belly. "It's like until I'm ready, I don't see. Here they are, all these stars, and I've been rushing so much, trying so hard, they've been invisible, but the difference isn't in the stars, it's in me. Until then I see crowds but I don't see faces, I see problems but I don't see solutions, I see how much I still want to do rather than celebrating what I have already done."

"But you're an optimist! I don't know anyone more so!"

"Even so, I fall short. Short of my ideal."

"So what then? How do you get around it?"

"I think I'll just let go ... here, try something with me. Want to reach those stars up there?"

"Okay. I'll play along. Yes."

"Think you can jump that high?"

"Um ... no."

"Well, then, shall we build a ladder?"

"We could, but what are we going to lean it on?"

"I see your point. Okay then. Close your eyes and hang on to the grass either side of your hammock. Got it?"

"Yes ..." Zach's voice was slow, questioning.

"Hold on really tight, really tight."

Zach pulled out a small tuft of grass, then widened out his grip and held on again. "Okay, I'm doing that, now tell me why."

"Because when you open your eyes, you'll see that we're not looking up at the stars, we're looking down at them, and if we don't hang on, we're going to fall. Open your eyes now."

Zach gasped, his fingers whitening. His face showed strain, his eyes bulging. "What now? Quickly!"

"Now ..." Jackie's voice became dreamy, hypnotic, "we let go ..."

"But ..."

"You said you wanted to reach the stars. Here's your chance. Close your eyes again if you're scared. Take my hand."

"I can't, I can't, I'll fall."

"Really it's okay. I'm with you. Here we go."

There was a long moment of silence. Zach swallowed and took a breath. "Only you, Jackie. With anyone else, lying out on the grass is a pretty safe thing to do."

38

Jackie stood at the top of the campground, looking out into the distance to where twinkling lights were scattered. Zach was asleep and she had come up here to be alone.

A tear slid down her cheek but she did nothing to stop it; she didn't even seem aware. This world she was entering was unfamiliar, and she felt a forward shock of homesickness. She was leaving behind the people who knew her, and who understood the life she had come from. Of course, they knew she was different, but she had been enough the same, too. Her parents' old friends still greeted her as if she were the seven-year-old, come looking for her older brother and maybe a biscuit and a glass of milk. This level of success was not what they were used to. She closed her eyes against the grief of anticipated distance. She longed for someone who thought they knew her, so she could dissolve into that fiction one last time.

"I'm not busy enough," she said, out loud. "I need something more to do."

Next day she visited the factory where the Life Kits were being put together. The machinists worked at lightning speed, turning out dozens of pieces of coloured fabric which were then collected by runners and fed to the assemblers. The folding mechanism had been perfected, and once they were put together the two men spun the strings with a practised twist more dexterous than anything Jackie had ever mastered. She felt oddly jealous.

"I'm not sure about the new colours."

"Market tested," Mason responded, without looking up from the report in his hand, although he swivelled his chair towards her. "There's a new demographic, not just those natural yoghurt hippies." He threw the papers onto the desk and looked up. "Besides, haven't you heard of colour therapy? Thought you'd be a fan with all your psychological do-gooding."

"Speaking of which, how is Pandora? Everything going well?"

The deflection worked. Mason's insecurity over Pandora made him much easier to talk to. "I wish you'd explain her to me, Jack. I'm out of my depth."

"She likes you. You like her. What's there to explain?"

"Does she? Does she like me? With her moods I'm never sure."

"Be sure, Mason, and get on with life. Running around trying to please her isn't going to make things any easier."

"Hmm ... She wanted to see you, by the way. They've got the results in from the public trial."

"Why didn't you say? That's fantastic!" She grabbed her bag and was running for the door.

He called out after her, in a crude imitation of her higher-pitched voice: "Thanks, Mason, you're doing a great job! I couldn't have done it alone." The door slammed behind her as if he hadn't spoken at all. "That's fine, Darling, my pleasure, don't you worry about it." He spun back to the desk and tried to start working again.

"Hey there!"

Pandora looked up at Jackie and smiled. "Hey, how are you?"

"You got the results? How do they look?"

"It's just the first batch, but look here. This group have clinical depression that had not responded to drugs. 45% have reported a significant improvement just during this initial six-week trial."

"Only 45%?"

"That's huge! Don't sound disappointed. These are drug-resistant patients who have been in therapy for as long as a year. This is a brilliant result! With a result like this you can start marketing."

"But how? 45%. How do we make that sound positive?"

"You say exactly that. You quote the study word for word. 'In a clinical trial of twenty-three drug and therapy resistant patients with depression, 45% reported a significant improvement within six weeks.' "

"Still doesn't sound that exciting."

"Well, you can just go away! I was buzzing until you got here. Is something up?"

"No. Everything's going well."

"And yet ..."

"Oh, okay, I'm a little down. I don't know why."

"I have just the answer."

Jackie looked up hopefully. Pandora threw her a Mood Meter.

"Very funny."

"I'm not joking. I know the inventor. They really work well."

Jackie sat in the car, weighing her options: Bob at work; Sandra at home; or … or Carlotta. She started the engine and headed for the little ex-state house.

She found Carlotta packing. "Gran? What's happening?"

"Hello, Darling. What does it look like?"

"But are you leaving? I thought you wanted to keep this place for ever."

"I did want to, but at ninety-three, forever looks more and more unlikely. I'm selling. Want to give that boy a start in life."

"But Zach doesn't need your money."

The old woman bridled. "Because he's got yours, you mean?"

"Well, yes. I've got more than I need now."

"You'd make him a kept man. It will end in tears."

"What makes you say so?"

"It is always so, a man kept by a woman."

"These are modern times."

The old woman's face set firm.

"You really don't need to sell your house. He wouldn't want it."

"He's been wanting me to move for years."

"But your security. You'll have nothing."

Carlotta peered closely towards Jackie's face. "What did you say?"

"I said you'll have nothing. If you sell the house and …"

"I thought …" Carlotta interrupted, grandly, "I'd like to Down Shift. I thought I'd try the nomad's life for a while. I've got a friend who has a campground. He's invited me to stay."

"Zach?" Jackie wondered, her voice singing the question.

"Not Zach. Craig." Her chest puffed out, proudly.

"Craig," Jackie repeated. She sank into a chair and looked at the carpet.

"He understands me. He's the biggest fan of my stories."

"I know. I know he is. Well, that's ..." Her voice petered out and she forgot that she had been talking at all. Carlotta bustled around her, continuing her packing, her throwing out. Finally she stood at the doorway, two suitcases in hand.

"You heading back out that way?"

Jackie's head jerked up. "Here, let me take those. What did you say?"

"I said, are you heading home, to the campground?"

Jackie shook her head. "No. Having dinner with Bob and Sandra first." Her mouth twitched. "Do you want to come? There's always plenty."

"And Zach?"

"He's out at Oxford. I came in on my own."

"You were looking for something. Did you find it?"

Jackie sniffed, repelling the symptoms of an on-coming cold. "No. I never found it. I'm always searching."

"But this is different."

Jackie didn't answer.

"This is different!" she said, more emphatically.

Jackie's head waved ambiguously, then her lips set. "I don't know." She looked around. The floor was littered with plastic bags, bits of old clothing. "What about the rest of this stuff?"

"It's all for the rubbish. Travelling light now. Zachie can take care of it. It's the least he can do."

Jackie shrugged, not taking the bait. “Well, I’m glad you’re coming out with us. Craig will be glad of the card partner.” She took the bags from Carlotta and stood back to let her walk out first.

“Just a minute, just a minute, I can’t go without Victoria.” She waddled back across the room and unhooked the brass cage from its bracket on the wall. The bird was crooning quietly as they walked down the path. Jackie could have sworn it was crying.

39

Jackie sat texting at the traffic lights.

"You're not supposed to do that when you're driving."

Jackie looked up at the lights. Still red. "I'm just letting Sandra know we'll be one extra for dinner."

Carlotta put her hand on the wheel, tugging it to the left. "You're not supposed to do that while you're driving. Pull over!"

Jackie sighed and put the phone into her lap, waiting for the lights to change then accelerating through the intersection.

"Now pull over."

"It can wait."

"No!" The old woman tugged on the wheel again. Jackie stood on the brakes and the car ground to a halt, diagonal to the curb.

"I'd rather you didn't do that."

"Now. Send your message."

In the rear vision mirror Jackie saw cars slow and weave around them. She sent a quick text rather than argue, however, then put the phone in the glove box, out of reach. As she backed onto the road and straightened up to continue driving, Carlotta opened the compartment and took the phone out again. "I've been thinking of getting one of these," she announced. "Craig thinks it would be good for me."

"Oh yes?"

"Yes. He thinks I've been too isolated. I need company, conversation."

Jackie glanced over. She reached out her hand and patted Carlotta's arm. "He could be right. You'll have company at the campground, though. Did Craig say what he's getting you to sleep on? The Life Kits only come with a hammock."

"Life Kit? What's a Life Kit?"

"It's what you'll be living in: tent, furniture, all designed to pack up small."

"Oh. That's what you call it? That's a good name. I'll be sleeping in a hammock, like everyone else."

"You tried a hammock before?"

"No. Why? Think I can't?"

"It's okay, I have a mattress if that's easier."

"I want the full experience, like everyone else. How am I going to talk to them otherwise?"

"It's up to you."

"So who's out there, then? Craig told me about the fishmonger and the queers. Who else?"

Again, Jackie glanced over. "You trying to wind me up?"

"Why?"

"We don't call homosexuals 'queers' any more. It's not polite."

"I'm not going to change just because the world's gone mad kowtowing to the thought police."

"Gran ..."

"All right. I'll behave. But I'll think what I like."

Jackie caught the edge of a mischievous grin as she pulled into Bob and Sandra's driveway.

"This where they live, is it?"

Jackie didn't bother to answer. Carlotta had a hand on her arm, stopping her from opening the car door. "You taking my Zach away, are you?"

"Think so. That okay?"

"It's all right. He wants to go. But you make my life a rollercoaster, giving and taking, giving and taking. You give me Sandra, you take my family with those recordings; you give me Craig and you take my Zach. Who'll be next? Will it be you, my Victoria?" She attempted to feed Jackie's mobile phone through the gaps in the bars. It was mercifully too big. Jackie watched, but didn't comment. "Give and take. Give and take. You're a strange one."

"I know. I know I am. But you know, everyone is just falling into place. I don't make them come and go, I just help them. They go as they choose."

Carlotta raised her eyebrows and slid her jaw out to the side to bite her top lip.

"Shall we go in?" Jackie asked. "I can see Sandra waiting."

The boys came running as they entered the house, then skidded to a halt in the kitchen doorway. Carlotta creaked down into a crouch, hands on her knees. "You can call me Gran, if you like. Aren't you a fine couple of boys."

They watched her, eyes large.

"Why don't you bring some of your cars to show me? I always loved cars and I never had one of my own."

They hesitated a second, then ran off, returning with an array of toys. They led Gran into the living room, chattering boldly to her about the excellence of the various vehicles.

Sandra raised her eyebrows.

"You don't mind me bringing her? I didn't fancy taking her to McDonalds."

Sandra laughed. "I'm glad to see her. She's a wise old thing."

"Eccentric."

"Maybe. I'm so looking forward to the time when I can get away with it. When I'm past caring what people think."

"Bad day?"

Sandra laughed again. "Oh, dear. Does it show?"

40

The plane took off and there was a sense of new life, of everything else left behind. Zach took Jackie's hand as she gazed out the window. He had questions, about schedules and plans, but she wasn't able to answer them.

"Mason'll take care of it," was all she could say.

Tim picked them up at Heathrow and took them to their hotel. There were a couple of days before the big show started. Mason would arrive the next morning.

"I just want you to come down tomorrow, for an hour or so, to check the stand and make sure we've got it set up the way you want it. Apart from that you can do what you like: sleep, sightsee, whatever."

Zach had the guidebooks out, ready to see and do everything. Jackie wafted along behind, getting lost amongst the crowds, causing them to miss trains and often looking in completely the wrong direction.

"Jackie, it's Buckingham Palace. Look. See the guards, see the balcony where the Queen waves out."

But Jackie was absorbing the sounds and the smells and the life, squirrels and birds and the flow of huge numbers of people. "See how they move differently? It's so precise. Stand on the right, walk on the left, pull your elbows in so people can get by, but if not, be patient, no problem. They're so polite."

In the wake of someone swearing at them for being slow at the turnstile, Zach wondered where she found her evidence. She simply didn't seem to see or hear anything unpleasant.

"He's probably just having a bad day. I'm talking overall statistics. You only count him higher because he stands out. He's one in a thousand. Look at her, and her, and him – all cheerful and pleasant."

Still Zach found it hard to shrug off, and became more and more weighed down by the repeated, if infrequent, episodes of incivility. They arrived back at their hotel, Zach exhausted, Jackie fresh and keen for more.

"Not tonight. I just need to sleep. Aren't you tired?"

"I slept on the plane, far more than you. Are you hungry? I'll go out and get something."

"No, sleep. Sleep, now." She helped him over to the bed, pulled off his shoes and rolled him so his head was on the pillow. She pulled a blanket from the end of the bed and laid it over him.

"I'm just going to go looking for dinner. I'll be back soon." And she went out into the London night alone.

The lights were dazzling. Even the Tesco Metro seemed exotic and she stood for fifteen minutes at the window of a laundrette watching the ballet of fifteen stacked machines turning. Finally an old man came to the window and scowled to scare her off. She smiled and waved and turned to walk towards a brighter row of shops and restaurants.

Zach was still sleeping soundly when she woke him next morning. "I can't wait any longer for breakfast. Come on, get up. I've got a surprise."

He showered, grumbling, and followed her down to the breakfast room, eating dry toast and drinking tea as she swallowed cup after cup of coffee and got more and more animated. "I found out we can get a train to Bath and be there in an hour! Come on! The Pump Room, the Assembly Rooms, the Royal Circus. Just like a Victorian novel!"

"When did you ever read a novel?" he muttered. "And I want to stay here. I want to see London."

She waved her hand. "It's too crowded. This way we'll work up to it. And you can see London while I'm at the show. Please? We'll go along to Earl's Court, as soon as you've eaten, then we can have the rest of the day, see the countryside, please?"

They wandered through the maze of stands to the Downshift showcase Tim had arranged and styled. Jackie nodded, suggesting slight alterations with wordless gestures. After fifteen minutes she stood back and nodded, walked several paces away in each direction in turn to experience how the visitors would see it.

"I like the posters. They give just the right feel - freedom and lightness."

"Thanks."

"And the screen - what's that for?"

"The DVD you had made, of the kits being used."

Jackie looked around, at the other stands, at the varied displays. "You think that will help?"

"I think so. We'll give it a try, anyway. If it's not popular, we'll can it. It has a quirky charm, though. My gut says it's right."

"Okay. So we'll see you tomorrow. What time?"

"Show starts at nine. We'll be here at eight."

"And say it again. What do you want me to do?"

"Answer questions. Demonstrate. Listen to what people are asking. Be yourself. They'll have interest in materials, fabrication methods. Those ones are mostly tyre-kickers – be polite but move them on as soon as possible. The serious ones will ask about weight and guarantees. And the best prospects, the retailers, will ask about supply lead times and colour ranges. Leave those ones to me. I'll ask if I need you."

Jackie nodded. "Okay. If that's all, we'll go. See you in the morning."

"Come fresh, bright and cheerful. The rest will fall into place."

41

Jackie told Zach to sleep in, come by the show later. She left him an Exhibitor's Pass on the bedside table and crept out early for breakfast. She was starting to go a little stir crazy, with not enough time on her own, and the show would be something else. Tim had described crowds like she had never experienced before.

She ate her egg and toast, pretending to read but really staring at the table cloth, tracing the pattern, trying to lose her self-awareness. She barely even heard the two-tone alpha state bleep. Fifteen minutes more and she stood up, deciding to walk to the show.

It was exactly as Tim described. For the first half hour, Jackie stood motionless, observing, noticing what people looked at, and their response. They were intrigued by the display; many conversations started about the concept of downshifting. Some had heard of it before, to others it was new. All were curious about the details.

When Jackie was ready, she stepped forward and took a chair from Tim's hands, demonstrating with three deft movements how it folded, packed and went up again. "Tim's the concept man; I'm the one who's lived this for five years. Here, let me show you the hammock."

Tim poked his tongue at her as the visitors stooped to watch how she shook it out. She turned her back on him to assemble the free stand. "You can use this separately, or the poles become part of the tent. See the special fittings here? They make it completely adjustable for height ..." But here she lost them. The DVD shouted into life. Tim quickly wound back the volume but they were irretrievably focused. "I had them, and you took them from me," Jackie whispered to Tim.

"Stop complaining. They're not pure Downshift material anyway."

"How can you tell?"

"Look at how they're glued to the box. They'll never give it up for the real simple life."

"I have a computer, iPod, phone. Are you going to discount me?"

"I should, but as you're the inventor ... But I don't believe you'd ever be trapped so absolutely."

She shrugged. "I don't know. Sometimes I'd come to and realise I'd watched three straight episodes of SpongeBob with my nephews. Not now, though, this lets me know when my brain goes numb."

Tim looked at the Mood Meter with new interest. "It tells you what?"

"Alpha state. It's the same as in other contexts, but without the benefits. Whatever is on goes in. No intelligent person wants that."

"Snob."

"I am not!"

"Be quiet! Look."

Jackie turned again, expecting to see the same couple. They were obscured by the crowd, however, many of whom were hooting with laughter.

"What's so funny?"

"Did you watch the DVD?"

"Not all of it. It wasn't ready. Mason only just got it produced in time to get here ... Where is he, by the way? He was supposed to be here."

"Delays, jet lag. He'll be here this afternoon. I said we could handle it."

"If all we have to do is watch people watch television, he probably needn't come at all. What are they laughing at now?" She pushed her way through to the front of the crowd to see the screen. A triple act was going on: Craig, Carlotta and Anna, reciting a deadpan rendition of their typical day. Did they mean to be funny? Did Craig somehow know precisely what he was doing? His face was straight but his comic timing was perfect, and he brought out the eccentric in Carlotta like a master – enough to be hilarious, skirting any true heresy in her thought or speech – and played her off Anna as if he had been training to entertain for decades.

The crowd was growing. The camera wandered into other tents, observed other activities, then periodically returned to the trio. Like punctuation, it accentuated, reiterated and in some cases wildly contradicted what was portrayed elsewhere.

"What did she say? What did she say?" It seemed they could decipher Craig, and even Anna, with her echo of his Cornish accent; Carlotta, however, with her New Zealand idiom, harsh vowels and obscure turn of phrase, had them guessing again and again. Now Jackie wanted to laugh; instead she found herself translating.

"It's her!" someone cried. "The inventor!" And a portion of the crowd broke away from the screen as if she were a celebrity.

"How did you do it?"

"Where did the ideas come from?"

"Do you live there, too, do you know them?"

And "She's so young!"

Tim turned off the screen when the half-hour program was over and some of the crowd loosened and drifted away. Jackie stepped back from the more persistent of them and grabbed Tim by the arm. "Can I get away for a while? I need a bit of quiet. What's wrong?"

"Nothing. You go. I'll be here."

"Tim ... tell me."

He rubbed his hair so that the tight curls stood up straight. "It just wasn't what I expected to happen. They were mesmerised, and now they've gone. We need a new game plan. We've got their attention, now we need to harness it. Tell you what, you take your ten minutes, then I've got an idea."

Mason was there when she returned, his head nearly touching Tim's as they continued deep in whispered conversation. Tim nodded towards Jackie, and Mason stepped back. He kissed her on the cheek.

"Hey there," she said, twirling out from his embrace. "You finally made it."

"I nearly didn't. Those damn DVDs. Only just ready in time, and then the box broke open at check-in. I was late as it was. They nearly didn't let me on the plane."

"Then delays."

"Yeah, delays. You got here okay then? You and what's-his-name." His eyes dropped in the face of her hostile expression. "Oh, all right, Zach. You and Zach got here okay? Where is he?"

"Asleep or sightseeing. I don't much care."

"Oh-ho! Trouble in Loveland. This is indeed good news."

"Stop winding me up."

"Still pretending you don't believe me ..."

"Is Pandora coming?"

"She can't get away. Sad."

Tim's loud throat-clearing startled both of them. "Charming though this reunion is, you did see each other only three days ago. Can we get on with the pressing issue?"

The two men turned to Jackie with speculating eyes.

"Do you think she's up to it?"

"Yes, I think she is."

"What?"

"Nothing, Darling. Just respond naturally, like you always do."

Tim pushed a way through the crowd, calling over his shoulder. "Give me ten minutes, then start."

"Start what?"

But Mason just grinned. Jackie folded her arms and sat down on one of the display chairs at the back of the stand. She looked at her watch and counted down ten minutes. With one eye on her, and making occasional conversation with browsers, Mason did the same. When the time was up, Jackie raised an eyebrow. Mason stretched his mouth as if he didn't know what was going to happen next. Jackie pointed at her watch. Mason walked over to the DVD player and pressed Play.

"Oh, no! Not that again."

Mason stood back, waiting. He seemed sceptical of the result. The three people who were there already turned to stare. Within a minute they were laughing. This attracted attention from people passing, and the group around the screen grew. And grew. And just like last time, they eventually recognised Jackie. She was surrounded, bombarded with questions, but no-one listened to the answers as the real-life comedy drew them in again. Jackie rolled her eyes, turning to exaggerate the movement for Mason's benefit, and got caught on camera, a local station recording an item for their news.

42

Respond naturally. This was Jackie's forte. She answered their questions, described her life, and led them to the screen, clearing a path through so they could film the audience from the front. As they were winding up the slot, Mason stepped in front of the camera.

"See what all the fuss is about," he said, and gave the company web address. Once the camera was off him he took out his phone, dialling fast.

"Who are you calling?"

"The web guy. He needs to get the DVD clip live, now."

Three days and the show was over. Jackie was high from the excitement of talking about her life, her invention, again and again. By the middle of the first afternoon they had put up a sign. "Next showing of Life Kit DVD:" and a time, spacing them with a thirty-minute gap. Crowds started gathering well before time, word of mouth spreading. Mason pushed Jackie towards one group and took another himself, to fill the time between showings with practical demonstrations of the product and his finely honed sales patter.

They returned to the hotel, Jackie talking a mile a minute. "Usually I need a break from people, but it's so much FUN talking about what you love doing, with a fresh audience every few minutes."

"I'll have to remember that DVD thing," said Tim. "It was great to have regular breaks from the usual expo intensity. Usually I'm shagged at the end of the three days, but with that, and the level of orders ... I'm up for a drink. Who's in?"

Mason put up a hand. "Hotel bar. Ten minutes. Be there."

Jackie went for a fast shower and change. Zach hadn't shown up at all today, and he wasn't in the room. She left him a note and returned downstairs.

"Nice dress."

"Thanks."

"Lover-boy not much of a one for night life?"

Jackie grimaced.

"Where is he? Having an early night?"

"I don't know. He's not there. He didn't leave a note."

"Shame. We'll just have to do without him."

Tim put a hand on Jackie's shoulder as her face crumpled. "Insensitive bastard! Leave her alone."

She wiped her eyes. "Maybe I'll send him a text, find out where he is." She took out her phone and her eyes widened as she looked at the screen. "Two missed calls. There was so much noise at the Expo. And a text." She pressed the button to open it, and read it out loud. "Met someone. Gone to Glasgow. Long story, I'll be back in a couple of days."

Mason chuckled and was silenced by another look from Tim.

"But ..." Jackie's brow flexed in and out of a frown. Mentally she scanned the room as she had seen it as she ran in and out, and noticed what she hadn't noticed before. Zach's stuff – his clothes and suitcase – were gone.

"He says he'll be back. It may not be what you think."

"What do you think I think?"

"Ah ... that it's a woman. He's gone off with a woman."

"I hadn't thought of that."

Tim and Mason exchanged a glance.

Jackie shook her head. "No. It isn't that, I'm sure."

Even Mason didn't have the heart to tease her. She caught his eye.

"What? He said he's coming back. He wouldn't do that if it were some romantic affair."

"Will you go after him?"

"I don't know where he is."

"You could ask him."

She licked her lips. "No. If he'd wanted me to follow, he'd have said." She flipped open her phone again and tapped out a text. 'Show over. Let me know if you need anything.' "There. Now it looks like I've got the evening free. Who's going to take me dancing?"

Tim was in his retail store the next day. He asked Jackie to come in, to talk to his staff and to adjust the displays as she thought fit. He called and had a screen brought in, and put it in the window. Even without sound the Life Kit programme drew a crowd.

"I think you need a screen inside, as well, and with sound. Do what you did at the Expo and have showing times. That was brilliant!"

She watched the staff handle the folding furniture and showed them faster ways to manage it, defter ways to expand and contract it. She watched with pleasure as their faces reflected the joy of success, snapping chairs open and closed as she did, and getting the hammock packing down to ten seconds flat. There was a section of the DVD where she demonstrated the same techniques. As it played she took them outside to watch.

Tim, in turn, watched her. "You're really great at this – a great teacher. Inspiring."

"It's easy. Natural."

"I'm heading out today to start delivering orders. I want you to come with me, do what you've done here."

Instinctively, she took out her phone to check the screen for messages. Nothing. "Zach ..."

"You can come back when he does."

"He said tomorrow."

"He'll let you know."

She compressed her lips and blinked wide. "Okay. Sure. I'll text him, and I can leave a message at the hotel."

As they went, from town to town, store to store, usually meeting with whomever had ordered at the show, Jackie began to ask questions as well as teaching. Who were their clientele? How did they see this in the market? She expected to hear about life changes, radical shifts in lifestyle.

"Nah, they're more of your luxury campers. Prob'ly use it once then into the garage. Still, it's money, init? Good price, these. Good commission."

For a few days she absorbed it. Then she took Tim aside. "I don't like it. This isn't what I wanted. I want to make a difference."

"Still not heard from Zach?" Tim's eyes were full of concern.

"What's that got to do with anything? I want people to see another way."

"I know, Love. But they have to be ready. You've shown them. They're watching the film by the thousand. You've said everything there. You have to let them make their own choices."

"But I want ... I want to make a difference."

"You are. Some people are getting it, doing it."

"Some people! I want more."

"Funny. You don't look ambitious."

Jackie's upper body jerked through a backward wave. "Ambitious? And what does ambition look like?"

"Oh, you know. Shoulder pads and calculators."

Jackie breathed a quiet laugh. She stood absolutely still for a long time: fifteen, twenty seconds, staring at the ground. "Ambition." She played with the word in her mind, in her mouth. "Ambition. Yeah, that feels right. That feels good."

"What?"

"Why shouldn't I be ambitious? What is it apart from following what you know is right, right to the end, as fast and effectively as possible? Isn't that what the ride of life is about?"

"The ride of life?"

"Yeah – you know! The full experience. Not sitting at home on the sofa but really getting out and living."

"And that's you?"

"Sure that's me. I never realised, but I'm different." Tim guffawed, then closed his mouth quickly. "I'm different, and this is how. Ambition. That's what it means."

By the end of a week they had made all the deliveries in the south west, complete with demonstrations. Tim was heading north, but as Jackie had still had nothing more than an occasional text from Zach, she refused his offer to go with him. "I'm going to Glasgow. Find out what is happening. I'll call you when I know what I'm doing."

"How will you find him?"

Jackie stared. "He'll tell me where he is when I let him know I'm there."

"Are you sure he's still in Glasgow?"

She shrugged. "I think so. He would have told me if he'd moved on."

"But ..." Tim looked at her face and closed his mouth. His expression was kind. "Good luck. I'd like to have you back here, visiting stores, whenever you're free."

She took the train back to London then caught the fast train to Glasgow, leaning her head against the window glass and staring out as the countryside flickered by. Absentmindedly she noticed the mood of the landscape, tamer and fuller than New Zealand's dramatic, large-scale geography. She liked it. It felt friendly and easy. But mostly, her mind was on Zach.

43

While she'd been busy she'd been able to put the mystery of his disappearance from her mind, assuming she'd see him in a day or two and he'd explain it. Tim thought it was something sinister, another woman, or some crime, but she was sure that wasn't it. She sent her feelings out towards him, wherever he was. The sense she had was of curiosity, intrigue, but not fear or loss.

"What's he up to?" she said into the glass.

"Sorry?" The passenger beside her who had been silent for three hours stretched and turned.

"Nothing. Just thinking out loud."

She had sent him a text to say she was coming, but so far, no reply. She checked her phone again. At the moment there wasn't even any coverage. An hour and a half to go. She slipped into an alpha state, confirmed by her Mood Meter. She was filled with the sense of Zach. He had been in the background while she focused on her work, but now she immersed herself in dreams of him. He didn't understand this, this ability to move from one mode to another, one focus to another. He didn't like it, it made him feel invisible, he said. Was that the issue? She squinted. Maybe partly. But he hadn't left to get attention, she was sure of that. Whatever he was doing was something he needed to do.

She sighed, remembering his words. "You don't want a partner; you want a part-time relationship, on tap when you need it, forgotten when you don't."

He was right, but what was wrong with that? She didn't understand why everyone wasn't like her in this respect. Jackie shook off the guilt-edged frustration and centred in on him again. He was lovely, sweet, kind and thoughtful. If only he wasn't so ... absolute.

The countryside outside was much less smooth now. She felt the train slowing through a level crossing in a small country town. Time to gather herself together and work out what to do next.

Jackie wandered the central city, getting the feel for it. It was diverse, with ancient architecture next to modern, affluent streets and jaded areas. Checking her phone every few minutes now, and sending Zach texts every quarter hour or so, she finally decided she should find somewhere to stay. She stopped outside a golden-stone guesthouse. Swallow Manor. Alan Crookshanks, proprietor. This would be as good as anywhere. She went inside.

The hall was cramped and over-stocked with furniture. Personality-filled carpet swirled through the entrance and up the stairs, creating a startling 3D effect that caused Jackie to miss the grey-cardiganed figure standing just inside the door.

"May I help you?"

She spun back round to face the man, losing her balance and using her small bag to regain it. Her arm swung close to his face.

"I'm sorry. I'd like a room, please, if you have one."

"I do. If you'd follow me."

The man creaked upstairs, the seat of his trousers shiny and mesmerising in front of Jackie's face. The stairs were narrow, and above the first floor they were tightly enclosed between close walls and low ceiling.

"You'll have come from London, then?"

"Yes. How do you know?"

"You can always tell." His voice was high-pitched within his diminutive frame. He took the stairs easily, but not fast. Jackie moved into his rhythm. "You'll have come for the weather, no doubt?"

"I, um ..." Jackie glanced out a small window at the grey sky, recalling a biting wind as she explored the streets.

The man cackled at her awkwardness, stepping through a door as he did so. They stood on a small landing, doors to left and right. "City or yard?"

"What?"

"City or yard? Do you like it quiet, or would you like to look over the street?"

"Oh, I, um ... can I see both?"

He took out a clanking bunch of keys, searching through for a long grey metal one which exactly matched his trousers. "This is city ..."

Jackie stepped through the low door, brushing against him as she passed. She felt his breath on her neck and resisted the urge to rub her skin, to remove the trace. The room was small, the ceiling low here, too. A stone window seat enclosed a casement, low on the wall and giving a view onto the street below. There wasn't much traffic, and the sound was muffled.

"And yard?"

They walked back through the landing into a dark room with a sloping black ceiling. The view was onto rooftops close behind, and no sense of movement.

"City, then, I think."

The man nodded. "I thought so. Flighty. Busy mind. Come from London."

Jackie ignored his muttering and carried her bag back through.

"Come down and check in once you've unpacked. Bathroom's on the floor above. Hot water before eight and after seven. And don't go wasting. City types." His voice receded down the stairs and Jackie closed the door behind him. She sank into a flowery chair and wondered what the hell she was doing.

"Zach, where are you? Time to come out of hiding. I'm here."

It was nearing eight o'clock, but still light, the day noticeably longer here than it had been in the south. She gazed at the floral-patterned bed for a moment, aching to just fall into it and sleep. She needed to make the trip back to the desk first, however. She didn't relish having her host come to find her. She looked at the door, realising he hadn't given her a key. What was the purpose of locking it at all? she wondered. She shrugged. One more text, one more check of the phone, then get it over with. Then she could rest.

The man came to the hall door as she tripped downstairs. He took a book from the desk and opened it to the last half page of entries.

"Name?"

"Jackie Fromm."

"Address?"

"Oxford Park, Oxford, New Zealand." Best not say it was a campground.

"And how long will you be staying?"

"I don't know."

"You don't know! You don't know! How can you run your life if you don't plan things?"

Jackie mumbled something about it depending on someone else.

"A young man, then. And not your husband." He sniffed through his long, narrow nose. Jackie feared for a moment he would throw her out. "It's £29 casual, £145 the week."

"A week, please, then."

"There's no return if you leave earlier."

"I won't," she heard herself saying, surprising herself. "The week." She handed him her credit card. He recoiled with horror.

"Oh no. Not those. There's a machine in the street, just a few doors down." He stepped away from her, speaking with distaste, and indicated the front door.

Jackie took a deep breath in and sighed it out in a gust. She pulled her feet reluctantly forward, further and further away from her bed.

Immediately surrounding the guest house were others, she hadn't noticed them before, only the one she had selected stood out. "I must be in the right place, then." She gave an involuntary shudder. One foot in front of the other. Credit card into the machine. Cash. Walk back. Pay. Stairs. Brave the antique plumbing. And finally, bed. The pillow was soft, the sheets crisp cotton. The clouds had cleared while she had been bathing. She gazed out the window into the glowing twilight and allowed herself to drift calmly to sleep.

She woke from eerie dreams. Reflexively she looked at the time before answering the startling ring of the phone. 2:30. Usually she turned it off before sleeping, because not all her New Zealand friends knew she was on the other side of the world.

"Hello?" Her voice rasped.

"It's me, Zach." He was whispering. "Where are you?"

"Glasgow."

"Where?"

She pulled herself up and awake. "I don't know. Central."

"Find out, please. I need to see you."

She rummaged in the small chiffonier which she could reach from the bed. There was a brochure for the guest house here. "West End. North Woodside Road. Swallow Guest House. Just near the bank."

"I'll be there soon. Wake up. We need to talk."

"Just a minute." What had the man said? "They lock the front door. Text when you get here, and I'll come down."

The stairs creaked as she descended. She prayed her host was a heavy sleeper. Even the hint of a young man had set him sniffing. What if he found her smuggling one in during the dead of night? She stifled a laugh. It was just like Bill Bryson.

Her heart was beating fast, knowing she was just about to see Zach, find out where he'd been. She opened the door and threw her arms around him, then stepped away quickly. "You've lost weight. And you're wet."

"It's a long story. Please, let me in."

44

Jackie sat on the bed watching him. She didn't know what to say. He towelled his hair vigorously, shivering, then wrapped the towel around his shoulders. He was only wearing jeans and a thin t-shirt. He looked frozen.

"Where is your bag, your clothes?"

"I lost it. I lost everything. Including my wallet."

She looked into his face for signs of despair, but instead there was a fiery fervour, a glittering sparkle.

"What have you been doing? Where did you go?"

"I decided to trace my family. My roots. Find out where I came from."

"Your family's Scottish?"

"Part of it."

"I don't understand. Why didn't you tell me?"

His face clouded and his nose twitched. "You were so wrapped up. You wouldn't have been interested."

"Zach ..." She proceeded cautiously. If she reacted angrily, she might not hear the story. "You said you'd be back in a couple of days. What happened?"

"I said. I lost my wallet."

"A week ago? What have you been doing? How have you been living?"

"On the street. It's not so bad. There's quite a culture."

"Zach!"

"Anyway, I couldn't come back, I was onto something. I found some cousins, they told me about the family, and today they took me out to the old family farm, where my ancestors on that side were servants."

"You couldn't have stayed with them? You had to live rough?"

Zach jutted out his chin. "See, I knew you wouldn't get it. You're missing the point. They were giving me what I needed. I wasn't going to ask them for ..."

"You could have asked me. Why didn't you ask me?"

Zach was angry now. "Will you listen to me! I had a week on the streets. Fine. I'm tough. Get over it. Do you want to hear the story or not?"

His voice was loud and Jackie looked nervously at the door. "Okay," she whispered. "Go on, tell me."

"There was this cottage, on the estate. They pointed it out across a valley. I said I wanted to see it, but the farm's owned by a different family, not welcoming. So I said, fine, I'd take my chances and walk across the fields. I just had to be closer, touch it. There was a pull I can't define. I just had to. So they went on, we agreed to meet at the pub a mile or so away in a couple of hours. It was so weird, the feeling I had, like a breeze across my skin, cold and enveloping at the same time. You know that feeling of being in exactly the right place?"

Jackie nodded.

"It was like my feet knew every footstep, I was jumping walls and little streams like I'd walked those fields every day of my life. I reached the cottage, it had a farmyard in front, and some barns. There was a pig in a pen, chickens wandering. I walked right up to the house, I was about to call out something, as if I expected to be expected. And then I stopped. It was eerie – no, not eerie, uncanny, like I was home, but not home. My heart was warm and strong in my chest, as if it was trying to speak to me. I knocked on the door. No answer. I stepped right up to the house and looked in the windows. It was just a normal domestic scene, normal domestic chaos. And my heart went cold. I turned and walked away, as if something was gone." His face fell after the enthusiasm of the walk.

"And what?"

"I don't know ... it's like there's more, but not there. Like I know something, and don't know it. I needed to go there, to be there, but what I was reminded of is not there. It's somewhere else. I have to find it."

"Where? With your relatives? Did you meet them, like you planned?"

"Yes. We had a drink. They brought me back to Glasgow, gave me dinner, then we parted. But it's not with them."

"Where then? Do you know?" She watched him closely, saw him gradually relax and smile.

He looked directly at her. "I think so. I think it's in me. And I'm ready to go home now. It's time to go home."

Jackie took the duvet off the bed and wrapped it round him, rubbing from the outside to warm him with the friction. He was shivering, and now his story was finished the life went out of him. "We need to get you something to eat. You're starving."

"No. I had dinner. I told you."

"But before that. How long since you'd eaten?"

"A couple of days, I guess. No more than a couple of days."

She watched him with concern. He moved over to the bed and flopped sideways, head on the bedspread, feet still on the ground. She lifted his legs and turned him a little.

"How did you lose your stuff?"

"Got mugged," he said, sleepily. "But it's okay, Jackie. It's okay." He seemed to be asleep for a minute, then lifted his head again. "But they took my Mood Meter. I'm sorry. I lost it. And I did miss you, even if you didn't miss me."

"I missed you, Zach! I wasn't worried. Maybe I should have been. But I trusted you."

"I lost the Mood Meter." His face became like a child's, bottom lip out, about to cry. "I was really sad. It was like losing you."

The conversation with the guest house owner the next morning was heated.

"He's not your husband."

"He's a friend, he's ill, I want him to stay."

"We don't have that sort of carry on in Glasgow."

Jackie stared him straight in the eye. "What sort of carry on?"

"Young people, not married ..."

"Yes, Mr Crookshanks?"

He floundered for words. "We don't have it!"

"He's not well. Do you want me to put him out on the street?"

"You can take him somewhere else. Down south, where they don't mind."

"Then you'll give me my money back? My £145."

His face creased and closed. His lips came up together in a compressed pout.

"Then it's all right if we stay?"

His face was stubborn, but he didn't say no.

"Now, I need to call a doctor. Is there one nearby?"

"Exhaustion. Perhaps a touch of hypothermia. Keep him warm, feed him soup, bread, get his strength up. He's young and healthy, otherwise. He'll be fine in a few days."

Jackie watched Zach sleeping, a glass of juice on the side table, a roll and butter on a plate, waiting for him to wake. She had Alan Crookshanks's grudging permission to use the microwave in the kitchen, to heat up some soup once he was awake enough to eat it. Her breathing was deep and even, matching his. She could feel he was getting better, there was none of the rasping hyperventilation that had punctuated the night. She looked out the window. Drawn by the noise of a siren she walked over and looked down into the street. The sunshine hit her face, a welcome surprise. She felt a smile come to her lips. It faded quickly. For the first time in her life, she was unclear what she wanted to do.

Tim was sending text after encouraging text, saying how well the sales were going, asking her to come back and help him on his circuit of the country. On the third day he phoned, insistent in his urging. Zach watched Jackie as she responded cautiously. His jaw came out as he listened to her half of the conversation.

"It's going fine, though. You don't really need me."

"It's going well, yes, brilliantly. But that doesn't mean it couldn't go better. You're a natural at this, and with the DVD, with people recognising you. There's so much you can add to what I'm doing. Another few weeks, months, maybe a year or two, you'll be set. Be able to buy yourself a mansion and retire."

Jackie looked over at Zach. His eyes were glazed and hard. She gave him a reassuring half smile.

"A mansion?"

"Yes! A mansion!" He seemed to think this would persuade her.

"Tim, do you not get the irony of that? I invented the Life-in-a-Box. Do you think I want a mansion?"

"Well, then, a sports car. Expensive clothes. Whatever you want. Just come and help me. We can do better together."

She nodded slowly, her face thoughtful, gently decisive. "Actually, Tim, you know what? You can handle this. You're brilliant at it, you love it. You don't need me. I'm going home."

Jackie and Zach got out onto the streets of Glasgow for the first time that afternoon. The sun was shining, reflecting off the buildings and the faces of the people. They strolled around the West End, had coffee at a café, visited the cathedral and the Gallery of Modern Art.

"Our week's up tomorrow. Do you want me to ask Alan to stay on?"

"No. I'm fine now. Thanks. I don't think I was very rational for a while. But like you said, it's time to go home."

"I'll phone the airline, we can take the train down tomorrow, leave the next day. But one thing?"

"Yes?"

"Can I meet your relatives before we go?"

"Sure. And I can say goodbye, too. They'll think I've fallen off the map, that I wasn't grateful."

INVENTOR

45

When they drove back into the hillside campground, the first thing Jackie noticed was that the gypsy camp of Life Kits had expanded to fill half the upper part of the hill. They had mushroomed in the gaudy colours she had never been sure about, adding a carnival aspect to the ancient landscape. The effect was accentuated by the green and red flash of parrot feathers, and the one-legged Cornishman dancing a jig in front of an illegal campfire.

"Craig," Jackie commented, dryly. He spun around, a beam on his face, and swung her off her feet.

"She's come home! The traveller returned."

"Looks like you've been revelling in my absence. What is this? A party? What's going on?"

"Don't you know? We're film stars. People have been coming looking for us. Tourists. You've put us on the map."

She smiled gently. "Well, you look happy."

"I am happy." He peered closer into her face. "But what about you?"

"I'm just tired. I'm going to get set up, then sleep. Hopefully for a couple of days."

Craig nodded down the hill to where Zach was leaning against the car, texting, then holding up his phone in vain for a signal. "See you've brought lover-boy back, then."

Jackie stared straight into Craig's eyes. "Why does everyone think they know better than me who and what I want?"

Craig raised his eyebrows and shifted his mouth sideways and back again. "He's a wet blanket. Even his grandmother says so."

"When you get her drunk, you mean. She's not the sort of woman you'd want to take literally, as a rule."

"Unlike you."

"Unlike me."

"Because you always say what you mean."

"Yup."

He smiled, and cupped a hand around her cheek. "That's why we love you. And that's why we want the best. Now, you'll need to be eating something. Here, I've cooked up a good Cornish stew."

"Cornish stew, eh? What's in that?"

"Well, should be seafood, but these around here don't know that. It's rabbit."

"From . . ?"

He jerked his head up the hillside.

"I think I'll pass, thanks. Come down, help me set up. Tell me the news."

Zach was sitting on the ground now, slumped back against the rear tyre of the car. He looked up as Jackie opened the boot.

"Hey, Honey. Tired?"

He stretched and stood up. "Yeah."

"Got enough oomph to go into Oxford and get milk and eggs? I should have stopped on the way through."

"Okay."

She threw him the keys and he came around to the driver's seat. There was a pause before he started the engine and drove slowly towards the gate.

"See? That boy. No gumption."

"He's peaceful." Craig snorted. Jackie shook her head. "He's just what I need. I need peace more than anything."

Jackie didn't sleep well that night. There was noise from the late night partiers and through the night an irregular stream of weaving feet making their way to the toilet block.

"Is it like this every night?"

"For the last few weeks," Craig responded. "But it's been mild. The first frost will see them off. I don't mind, it's been a very good season. The busy campgrounds are noisy. That's just the way it is. I've done well out of it." He fingered one of several chains around his neck. A medallion lay against the hair of his chest, in the V of a Lycra shirt that hugged his body.

"I noticed this yesterday – jewellery, new clothes – what's that about?"

"Nothing wrong with showing off my wealth. The ladies like it. And I don't trust banks."

Jackie's eyes boggled. "Is that gold? Solid gold."

Craig nodded proudly. "And I've taken up cycling. Let me show you my beauty."

He went back to his hut and wheeled out a minimal racing bike, silver and gleaming. He looked at it as if it were a favourite child.

"Nice. And the leg goes well on it?"

He went back into the hut and brought out a streamlined, not immediately identifiable object. "Got a special one, specially designed. You should see me ride with this one!"

"Wow! Cool!"

"Want me to show you?" He bent down to un-strap the leg he was wearing. Jackie put out a hand. "Tomorrow. I've got to get into Christchurch now, meeting Pandora to look at the data she's collected and work on reprogramming the Mood Meter. Zach's still asleep. Will you tell him where I've gone, let him know I'll be back tonight, and tell him to call from your land line if he wants anything?"

46

Pandora opened the door immediately in response to Jackie's knock. "I've been waiting for you. There's so much to do." She was smiling and eager, which contrasted with her habitual cool cynicism. "These results are amazing. I've started writing them up, but I want to do more. I want to take it a step further. I'm seeing patterns in the data that suggest another level of possibility. But you'll see it better than me telling you. Come and look?"

Jackie's eyes were already on the screen as she absentmindedly pulled up a rolling chair and sat down. "What's this?" She turned to look at Pandora.

"I know. Radical, huh? I was staring and staring at the data, and this pattern jumped out at me. So I charted it separately. It's mind-boggling."

"And what are the stats?"

"For the 45% who show the initial response, nearly 90%."

"Wow!"

"Yeah!"

"I hadn't anticipated this. It's brilliant!"

"I didn't think of it, either. It was just there."

They both turned as the door opened behind them.

"My two favourite women."

"Hey Mason. You're back." Jackie glanced at Pandora, who was half raised out of her chair, her features closing over a briefly hopeful expression. Pandora pulled back her arms which had been reaching out to him in greeting.

"It's such a shame you left. We were doing so well."

"We'll do well without me there. I'm not necessary. I'm an inventor, not a salesperson. Come and look what Pandora's found, for the Mood Meter."

He waved this suggestion aside, sitting one buttock on Pandora's desk. "Tim thinks we can do twice as much business with you doing your thing, talking to retailers, training them, with all that passion bursting out. It's thrilling."

Out of the corner of her eye Jackie saw Pandora turn back to the computer, shoulders slumping.

"Tim does fine on his own. Everyone loves him. He's too modest."

"Still, your part of the bargain is to do your share of promotion."

"Get me a television interview. I'll do an ad. But I won't spend my life going door-to-door."

"Our contract ..."

"Will you shut up! I'm trying to tell you, Pandora's had a breakthrough. This is going to take the Mood Meter to a vastly huger audience. We're better with me working on this than as a sales puppet on a string."

Jackie waved him forward. Reluctantly, Mason took a few steps towards her, leaning over her shoulder, hands in his pockets, to peer at the screen. He was almost touching both her and Pandora. Pandora pulled back, then stood up. Mason settled himself on her chair without looking at her. "So what am I looking at?"

"It's the trend over time. We hoped that we could work with depression, bring people back to an even state, to a normal level of function. But something else is happening. They're getting happier and happier, like they're training themselves towards some sort of super mood state."

"So?"

"So this means, not just working with dysfunction. We can sell this to healthy people as well. We just trebled our market."

Now Mason was interested. "Trebled?"

Jackie nodded.

"And you came up with this?" He turned to Pandora, looking at her properly for the first time. "Well, who's my darling girl then?"

A spasm crossed her face, and her brow creased. She took a deep breath, and then another. "Patronising bastard. Get out!"

Jackie walked with Mason across the car park. "So we'll need another trial, another separately conducted study, this time starting with a broader sample. Another couple of months. But we can work on the marketing and packaging now. I'm sure it will show what we expect. Actually I should have seen this coming, but life's been so up and down for me, externally, that I didn't have the base to work from myself."

"I still don't get what I did wrong. I was just teasing. Why's she so upset?" He stopped walking. Jackie opened her mouth, frowned, and turned towards him.

"Do you really not know?"

"I was just, you know, playing."

"Well, let me spell it out for you. You and she are an item. She loves you, and you went away for a month, as far as she knows with me. You've been making jokes about you and me since I met her. Then you come back, ignore her, and start with the jokes again. She's hurt, and she has every reason to be."

"But I thought women liked to be kept guessing. If I'm too easy, too eager, she'll get bored."

"Do yourself and her both a favour. Give her the opportunity to get bored. And then see. It might not be as boring as you think. And I'd really appreciate it if you stopped making cracks about you and me. I think sexual harassment is probably grounds for dissolving our partnership, and financially that would be a really bad thing for you."

"Sexual harassment!"

"Whatever you want to call it. Stop playing games, Mason, with me and with her, and for your own sake, with everyone. It's inefficient, it's boring, and I'm not impressed."

Mason held up his hands in mock surrender. Jackie turned from him and walked away.

47

Craig was right. The next week there were three frosts and the campground emptied. The only ones left were Jackie, Zach, Carlotta and Craig.

Jackie felt her shoulders relax as she listened to the silence. Carlotta was less happy, however, grumpy about losing her audience, although she wouldn't admit it. She dressed her dissatisfaction up in criticism of the weak nature of people in general.

"Gran, you need to go, too. It's too cold. And it's dangerous coming down those steps when they're icy."

"You can move my tent down here, if you like, but I'm not leaving. This is my home now." Her face set, the creased surface looking like weathered stone. Zach's jaw came out, ready for a fight, but Jackie put a hand on his to restrain him.

"I've got another idea. You'll be down here playing cards with Craig anyway right? Most evenings, at least."

Carlotta looked at Craig and they both nodded.

"And Craig, the next step was to enlarge your hut, build you something bigger – now you're a successful man of the world."

He puffed his chest out and nodded again.

"Well then, let's do that, and then Carlotta can take the second bedroom, insulated and heated." She looked from one to the other, feeling Zach with his breath held next to her.

"When the crowds come back I'll want to be up there again." Carlotta spoke belligerently, her nose wrinkled.

"Sure, fine. Once the weather's good."

"Well, all right. This young man needs some looking after, some fattening up." She cackled and punched Craig on the arm.

"And for me, I think maybe it's time I moved on again." Jackie gazed out over the plains, towards the sea.

Zach stiffened beside her.

"You can come too, of course."

When she didn't feel him relax she turned to him. His face was hard, a reflection of his great-grandmother's. "No. Just no. I'm not leaving Gran and I'm not moving again."

Jackie sat at Sandra's dining table watching her nephews drive cars around a plastic play floor, pseudo-engine noises roaring. When only one voice grunted, it was loud. With two it was cacophonous.

"It's so peaceful here," she joked.

Sandra stretched her mouth. "I'm sorry."

"No, actually, I mean it. The simple joy of children. I wish everyone I knew was still a child. Adults are so messed up."

"Yup. All of us. Except you."

"I'm not so sure about even me, now. Life was so simple when I worked on my own, lived on my own. I feel so responsible now, for so many people. I just wish they'd take responsibility for themselves."

"We try."

Jackie put her hand out to her sister-in-law. "I didn't mean you. Besides, you're doing well now. You're healthy and you look great."

"I'm worried about Bob, though."

"Bob? Why?" Jackie sat up straight, her eyes opening wider.

"It's business. Money's been tight. And then ..."

"What? Don't mess around not telling me. Be straight."

Sandra inhaled and froze. Her voice came out on a gusty exhale. "It's that girl. Janine. He talks about her all the time."

"What sort of talk?"

"Nothing specific. Just general, enthusiastic talk. Things she said. What she does with her life, how glamorous she is."

"And you're jealous."

"That's our Jackie. Straight to the point, as always."

"Do you think there's anything going on?"

"No. But I think he's half in love with her, and he doesn't know it."

"But he's fully in love with you, and he does know that."

Sandra stared and bit her lip as involuntary tears formed. "Intellectually I know that, but emotionally ..."

"Oh, God!" said Jackie. "Leave it to me. I'll talk to him. Sort it out."

"It's not your problem. It's just nice to have someone to talk to. I feel better already."

"He's my brother. I owe it to him not to let him mess himself up."

When Jackie walked into Bob's office, she could feel immediately something was different. He turned to her, his face lined and grave. When he saw her, he broke into a smile. "Hey there! I wasn't expecting you today." She hugged him, and he held on a little longer than usual.

"So what's happening? No improvement in sales? How is Janine working out?"

"She does a great job, works hard, she's fantastic!" His voice was enthusiastic, but there was strain underneath.

"But . . ?"

"But you're right. No change." He bit his lip.

"Out with it. I haven't got time or patience for wheedling it out of you."

Bob hesitated, then wrapped his arms around her again, resting his head on her shoulder. He squeezed her tight for a few seconds. She felt him drawing strength from her, and gave it gladly. The time came for a natural release, and he let her go. "I don't know how long I can keep going. The overdraft's bigger than it's ever been, and things keep getting worse. I think I might have to sell."

Jackie nodded.

"You're not shocked? Or upset?"

"Should I be?"

"This means I'm a failure."

"No it doesn't. It just means you're letting this go. Your heart was never in it."

He leaned back against his desk.

"So what are you going to do?"

"Just like that?"

"Sure. Why not?"

"I've been doing this for eight years. It was Dad's dream. His life's work."

"*His* dream. *His* life's work."

"So then I can't let it go. It'd be like ... like I didn't love him."

"No. It wouldn't. He'd understand. He never would have wanted it to be a burden."

"But what will I do? How will I even pay back what I owe?"

"I can help you."

"No." His voice was firm. He folded his arms.

"Bob, listen to me." His face set, stubborn. Jackie was reminded of Carlotta and sighed. "You've done everything for me. I know how hard it was for an eighteen-year-old to have sole charge of his thirteen-year-old sister. I've said thank you, but I've never been able to repay you. Let me do it now."

"No."

"I have money. What else am I going to do with it?"

"You could buy a house, get yourself some security."

She stared at him. Her eyebrows flicked upwards sceptically.

"Oh, all right. I know you don't want that. But I already feel like a failure, this would make it worse."

"Imagine this, Bob."

He waited. "Yes?" he said, finally, impatiently.

"Imagine being able to close the doors here, walk away, done. No debt, no responsibility, finished. Imagine if you could leave today and never have to come back. How would that feel?"

He took a deep breath in and let it out, his hands stretching out either side of him on the desk. He closed his eyes. "Wow. Fantastic."

"So let's do it. Maybe not today, there are probably things you need to do, orders you need to fill, and I'll talk to Mason to see if there's any chance of selling the business as it is. But you can let it go, right now, emotionally. Relax. How much is that overdraft? I'll pay it today. And it will make my day. It really will. To be able to do something real for you, after all these years of you looking after me."

He smiled, sniffed, then his shoulders pulled back tense again. "What about Janine? I'll have to let her go. I can't do that. She loves this job."

"Okay, here's the thing. I was going to talk to you about that ..."

48

Jackie left her car outside Bob's office and they drove home together. As they were turning into the driveway, Jackie felt a change in him. He switched off the ignition but instead of getting out of the car he turned to her.

"Do you really mean it? You can help me get out? And you think it's okay?"

She reached over and took his hand, letting him read the compassion, acceptance and love in her eyes. "More than okay. It would mean so much to me to see you relaxed and happy."

He smiled, halfway between gratitude and disbelief. "Well then, let's go tell Sandra."

Jackie held back as her nephews hurled themselves at their father. He crouched down and hugged them, laughing in a way she hadn't heard for months. Sandra looked over, puzzled. He stood and reached out to her, and she came and nestled in at his side. "What?"

"We're going to sell the business. Jackie is going to help me out."

"Oh!"

He hugged her tight. The boys pulled at his trouser legs. "Go get the cars set up," he suggested. "We'll have a race before dinner."

Their footsteps thundered off through the doorway and into the hall. Sandra looked up into Bob's face. "Are you okay? What are you going to do?"

"I don't know. Get a job. Somewhere I can work a forty hour week and actually get paid at the end of it. Somewhere the people are fun and enjoying life. Somewhere I can feel like I'm making a difference. I don't know who'll hire me, but someone will."

Sandra opened her mouth to speak, then closed it again. Bob squeezed her closer again for a moment. "It will work out. I know it will. I'll find something."

Jackie cleared her throat. "Actually ... I was thinking ... in the longer term, or just while you look for something else, you could come and work for me."

They turned to stare at her. She shrugged. "The factory's expanding, so that needs to be overseen. And then the management. You know I'm no good with the day-to-day."

"But I've been a financial disaster! Why would you think this would be any different?"

"You've always been great with your staff. You make sure they're happy, and their productivity is great."

"Yeah. Just they never had enough to do, and I never had the heart to fire them. God, I'll have to now, I can't bear the thought."

"Offer them to come to us. We need more workers, and yours are good. Your problem was marketing, and following up payments. You wouldn't have to do that. Just fill the orders that come in, and keep the place cheerful. You'd be great."

Dinner was noisy and happy. Bob's spirits had rebounded from the weights that had held them down and he was boisterous, winding up his sons and daughter to shrieks of laughter. Sandra rolled her eyes as she tried to herd them through to bed. "I'll take them," Bob offered.

"No. If you do they'll never sleep. You sit here with Jackie and chat."

He put the kettle on. "What can I get you?"

"Hot milk. I'll make it." She poured milk into a mug and set it spinning in the microwave. Bob had his back to her, so it wasn't until he turned with his instant coffee in his hand that she saw he had been crying. "What is it?"

"God, it's just the relief. It's really sinking in." He brushed his sleeve across his face and smiled. "With all this new wealth, you should do something for yourself. I'd feel bad if you wasted it all on me."

Jackie ignored his self-deprecating words, and the falsely jovial manner. He would settle into the new state of affairs in his own time. "Actually there is something I've been thinking about."

"Yes?"

"I'd like a new car. Would you help me find one?"

"Sure. I'll have a look in the paper tonight."

Jackie shook her head, turning as the microwave dinged. "No, not second hand. New. Let's go around the dealers tomorrow." She tested the temperature of the milk and put it back in for another round.

"A new car? But second hand is ... new cars lose so much value, just by driving them off the lot."

"Bob, I'm rich now. I have almost nothing I want to buy. I want a new car."

He coughed. "Well, what? A Toyota. Maybe one of those new Chinese brands, they're great value."

"Na-uh. I was thinking of a Porsche."

49

Jackie took Bob to visit Mason, to ask his advice. He looked over the books, the accounts for the last four years.

"It's the wage bill that's been killing you. You just didn't have enough sales to support it."

"But we got busy each year, just before Christmas. I needed the staff to keep up then."

"I can see the pattern. But it would have made sense to hire casual staff."

Bob slumped in his chair.

"Look, you've got good, steady orders, not growth, but a reliable revenue stream. Keep it going, just reduce the staff."

Bob shook his head. He looked like he was going to cry.

"Not as it has been. Jackie's right, you're better used with us. We'll transfer over the phones and take orders through our system. That way you don't have to pay a receptionist. We can tie in an email marketing campaign with your existing customers, more or less automated from year to year, and targeted just at your peak times. You can have one or two guys stay on in the factory and build the stock. When you're busy, you can borrow staff from us, if we've got excess capacity, or take on temps that your guys can manage.

Easy. You'll have your salary here, and you'll see a profit from this too. And you won't have to shut it down. There's no need. It was your parents' business, right?"

Jackie and Bob looked at each other. "Yeah."

"So that's good. It's a good little business. Let's see how it goes. In the meantime, get the phones switched over, talk to our operators, and start here on Monday." Mason stood up and gestured wide, making it clear the meeting was over. As Bob walked through the door, Mason put a hand on Jackie's arm. "We need to talk. Can you stay a few minutes?"

She stood, waiting for him to speak.

"I've been thinking about what you said. It doesn't work for me. You're the face of the company. The poster girl. Freedom with her Life-in-a-Box. We need you out there promoting. Doing interviews. Living life out loud, for the cameras."

"I don't want to do that. I explained."

"Maybe. But this is business. With you in the media we could potentially grow ten times as fast. Ten times! Let me paint you a picture."

Mason was charismatic, persuasive, as he described the world of enormous success. "Think of all the extra lives you'll change. Freedom for the people of the world. We need role models, not movie stars with dysfunction and addiction, but someone choosing a life and making it real. That's you. You're inspiring. So inspire people. Tell them. Let them see how it's done!"

"Mason ..."

"I know you can see it. You said you were searching for the ultimate invention, one that very, very simply changes lives. This is it!"

"I don't know. It seems like for most of our customers it's just another fashion trend. Something else to store in the garage and forget about."

"I know. We've known that from the beginning. For some. But what about the others? The 5%, 10%, maybe even 30%, for whom it truly means the start of a new life. What about them? And who can say, even with the others, that it isn't the start of a new freedom? They try the nomad's life, and find it isn't for them. But by clarifying that that isn't it, they get a step closer to what truly is for them."

Jackie looked into Mason's face, alive and passionate. She sighed.

"Think of all the lives you could change." He watched her closely, eyes alight.

"God, you! How do you do that?"

"You know I'm right. It's not just about you."

"But I just ordered a Boxster – red, new, gorgeous."

"All the better. We'll get some footage of you in it before you go."

"Go?"

"I've set up an interview in Auckland on Thursday. Then I thought we'd hit the States."

Jackie met with Pandora the next day to work out the next course of action for the Mood Meter, and discuss how they could work long distance. "I'll have email, a phone. We'll keep in touch."

"But it's not like being here. We know that from before."

"I know. But you know Mason. He gets fired up and he's irresistible."

Pandora stiffened in her chair. She looked fixedly out the window.

"Not like that! Pandora, can I give you some advice, straight out?"

She turned, watching Jackie out of the corner of her eye.

"Can I?" A minimal nod. "Mason adores you, and he keeps you hopping because he's insecure. Don't take any notice. Live your life as if he'll be with you forever, not as if at any moment you're expecting him to leave."

"But he might. He's way too handsome. He's always been out of my league."

"Oh, well then, give up. Fire him now before he fires you."

"Not funny."

"Then get over it. He might leave. If he does, you'll survive. In the meantime, what's the point of a relationship if you don't enjoy it? Relax. Assume he loves you. Have a good time with it. And at the same time, build up the rest of your life. Decide to be happy. Put on one of those Mood Meters yourself and get in a good mood." She watched as Pandora's thoughtful face became more and more unhappy. "Look, it's all about how you see yourself. If you know you're beautiful, he'll think so, too."

Pandora fixed her eyes on Jackie, her head on one side.

"Act as if you're the sexiest, most beautiful woman, and he's lucky to have you."

Pandora looked up into the corner of the room, then back at Jackie. Her forehead creased with concentration. "Could I really do that?"

"You're an intelligent woman. What do you think?"

50

Sandra drove Jackie to the airport. "This doesn't feel right."

"I know. You're right, I know."

"You're happy here. You should stay here. And what about Zach?"

"I asked him if he wanted to come with me, but he said 'no'. I've told Mason, three weeks, a month maximum. Then I'm coming home. I might go again, but at least I have that timeframe to cling to. At least I know I'll be back."

"How did he take it? Zach, I mean."

"Like I did. He's sad. We're both sad. We belong together."

Sandra opened her mouth to answer, but was interrupted by the chiming bongs of an announcement. They waited, listening. A delay. Ice on the runway. They were trying to clear it.

Jackie's face fell. "It'll be cold out at the campground tonight."

"Zach's staying out there?"

"He won't leave his gran. It's driving me crazy. I feel trapped every way."

"So what did Mason say, to persuade you?"

"That I could change lives. It's what I've always wanted. And this is my chance. Except ..."

"What?"

"Something tells me it's not this. It's something else."

"And yet you're going."

"Yes. I'm going. It's the only way to find out for sure."

Mason had signed a deal with a US distributor, and they were exhibiting "Life-in-a-Suitcase" as part of their trade show circuit. "We're trying for TV coverage. This is not standard stuff for the States, where bigger is usually better. You'll stand out as different."

Jackie got on fine with the staff on the stands but they were employees, hired to do this one thing. They didn't own the company, they were paid on commission and for them it was just a job. They were young, efficient, and they didn't have families they missed. Jackie was lonely.

The television cameras appeared as before. Without the DVD to liven things up, Jackie had to generate the mood herself, and found she often spent most of her time on air explaining what the Life Kit was.

"You mean everything is in here? Everything? You can live just out of this one case? Really?"

And Jackie would nod, and her time would be up.

Day after day, hour after hour, she had the same conversation over and over again.

"They don't get it, Mason. I don't think they're ever going to get it. I want to come home."

"It just seems like that. It's working. We have more orders than ever before."

"I feel like a freak."

"It's just unfamiliar. You're making new converts. It just takes time."

"You make it sound like a religion."

"Well, isn't it? Jackie preaching freedom."

"If you were here, I'd punch you. Maybe I'll remember when I see you next week."

"Here's the thing. There's another show. Tuesday, Wednesday, Thursday. This one's different – an inventors' show. You'll be doing it on your own, just you and the one product. It's a different world, a different vision. After that you can come home, I promise."

Mason was right – the inventors' show was different. People came to Jackie's stand knowing who she was. She could begin from a point of understanding and let her enthusiasm show. It seemed her Auckland interview had been played on an inventor programme here, and people had seen it. These were kindred spirits, and she wanted to get off the stand and meet them. Fortunately several of them came to her, asking questions, taking an interest, getting deep into her philosophy of changing lives. She found herself voicing her frustration, that people didn't get it faster.

"You've got to give them time. People take their own time."

Jackie looked into the wise old face. The man looked like Edison, and was just as phlegmatic.

"I guess I'm just impatient."

He shook his head. "No. It's not patience you need, it's faith."

"What do you mean?"

"I mean, if you were sure it was going to happen – really certain – you'd be able to wait."

She went to dinner with the old inventor, Victor, and his friends that night, a group of experimental hobbyists who had had successful careers and were coming back to this passion in their retirement.

"I wish I'd been like you and done it, full time, when I was younger. Imagine what I could have done if I'd spent forty years following this. So what's the next thing for you? What's the next invention?"

Jackie started. "I'd almost forgotten to think about it, I'm so frustrated not to be there doing it." She explained the Mood Meter, then reached down to take hers out of her bag. "I don't wear it at the moment, because it makes me homesick. But here it is."

The men turned it over and over in their hands, taking it one by one, mouths falling open. They turned to stare at her.

"What was it you said you wanted?'

"A simple way to change people's lives."

"Then what are you doing here, with that tent thing?"

Jackie took the Mood Meter back from Victor's friend, short and round-faced and eager. "You think this is it?"

The five men nodded in unison. Jackie groaned and put her head on the table. "I knew it. I knew it. I should have listened to my heart."

51

Zach was at the airport to collect her. She fell into his arms. "Take me home? I just want to go home and never leave again." Zach pulled back, his mouth open to speak, but he stopped when he saw her face. "Jackie? What is it?"

"I missed home and I missed you. It was awful."

"But you're fine. You're always fine. You're always so strong!"

She laughed, near hysterical. "People keep saying that. Don't you get me at all?"

"You know I do."

She went quiet, sobering quickly. She put a hand on his face. "Yes. I know you do. That's why I picked you. Please, take me home."

She left her cell phone off, and refused to call Mason. "I'll see him in my own time." On the third day after her return, he appeared at her tent. She was still in her hammock, eyes closed, though it was after midday.

"Come out. I need to talk to you."

"No."

Zach stood warily at the entrance, holding the tent flap open. Mason took a step inside and Zach let the flap fall.

"Jackie ..."

"You can talk to me here. I'm not getting up. I'm never getting up."

"People want to see you. We need to talk about new additions to the Life-in-a-Box. A TV stand for the American market."

Jackie snorted.

"You can do it. You know you can."

"Physically, yes. Morally, no. I am not adding a TV stand to my Life-in-a-Box."

"They want it."

"Well, they can't have it."

Mason let the subject drop. "There's something else. Mike. Has he shown up here? He's been looking for you, frantically. He says he's discovered something, but he won't tell me what."

Jackie lifted her head and looked from Mason to Zach and back again. The hammock swung gently with her movement. Zach's face was thunderous. "What? Did he give you any clue?"

"Not apart from he said he's been trekking in India – did you know that? He hadn't told me."

Jackie looked thoughtful. "I wondered why I hadn't seen him, but there's been so much going on. I wonder what it is."

"Then I suggest you turn your phone on, you'll probably find out. God, I can't talk to you when you're swaying. I'll wait outside."

Curiosity levered Jackie from her bed. She pulled on a jumper and stumbled down the hill to the toilet block, shivering in the early spring air. On the way back she noticed more clear land beyond the current site, and a flat concrete pad at the edge of the leased tent site.

"What's that?" she asked Zach, still ignoring Mason.

"New toilet and kitchen. Craig's been taking bookings all winter, the old area was booked full by mid-June."

Jackie raised her eyebrows. "There goes my dream of peace and quiet. Shouldn't he have asked me? We're still partners."

"Guess he thought you were busy. Would you have said no?"

"No. I suppose not."

Mason cleared his throat. Jackie turned to him. "Okay. Mason. Here's the thing ..."

They argued for the better part of an hour. Zach went for a walk, and Craig and Carlotta were soon on the sidelines, both loving a good altercation. The two birds sat side by side on Craig's shoulder. Carlotta occasionally cheered when Jackie or Mason made a clear point. Craig pulled her up a chair and they both sat slightly apart, leaving Jackie and Mason the space around the table like boxers in a ring.

"I thought you got it! To maximise return we need to market."

"Of course I get it! It's a question of priorities. And this isn't it, for me, any more."

"So what is?"

Jackie held up her wrist.

Mason shook his head. "Yeah, it's a clever idea. But it's not straightforward. The marketing is muddy. We don't know what we can claim for it and get away with. We're not doctors, and if we claim we can cure mental disease, we'll be up for all sorts of law suits."

"You have to let people make their own choices, Mason. Aren't you sick of having lawyers and politicians tell you what you can do? Don't you want the freedom to decide for yourself?"

"I do, yes. But the general population ..."

"Are underestimated, and underestimate themselves. I want to help give them back personal responsibility."

"It's a risk."

"You're a businessman. Estimate the risk and mitigate it. We don't have to make clear claims, we can give ideas, possibilities, testimonials, and let people go from there. It works, and people should be able to have it if they want it."

"But we've already got a winner here. If you'd just keep going with the Life Kits, you can be set for life."

"Set like a jelly, or set like concrete? I'm twenty-two. I don't want to be set for life. And I'm an inventor. I need to keep inventing. Who knows what will be next? I need time for that. And headspace. This marketing is killing my headspace."

"It's just a little while longer ..."

"No."

"Our contract ..."

"Mason!" There was a warning in her voice which made him lean back, then get out of his chair and walk to a little distance. Craig huffed, delighted, and Carlotta gave a little cheer.

"So what are you saying?" Mason asked, finally. "What do you want to do?"

"I want a compromise. I want to take the Mood Meter as far as it will go, and I want you to find a way we can do that. Talk to the lawyers, talk to Pandora and find out how far we can go. It's time to get it produced and out there. We can refine it later. And I want a month off, to work on new ideas."

"What new ideas?"

"If I knew that, we wouldn't be having this conversation. You're not like me, you can work in response to outside stimulation. I need quiet, for rest and reflection. My ideas don't come step-by-step, like a staircase. They come all at once, out of the silence, a giant leap."

"A giant leap."

"That's the idea. Then there's the implementation, the creation and refinement. And then the selling. That's where you come in. And earlier, because there's flexibility in the physical realisation. You might want to market test for colour and size, whatever."

"Colour and size of what?"

"I don't know!" She was shouting, exasperation overflowing. "That's my point!"

Mason pulled his lower lip over his upper one and stared out into the distance. His hands were in his pockets and he stood perfectly still. For five minutes they all watched him. Carlotta began to fidget, and Anna took off from Craig's shoulder and made a wide circle overhead. Finally Mason turned. "Okay. I think I'm starting to get it. Although I don't get it – you're not like me." Jackie laughed. "Okay. Make me a coffee, and then I'll go."

52

Zach returned to watch Mason drive away. At the last second, Jackie ran after him. "Send Mike to see me. I want to know what he's found out." She turned to Zach. "Take me into town? I'd like to see Bob, see how he's doing, and pick up my car." She rubbed her hands together. "I so want to pick up my car. I've been dreaming about driving it all the time I've been away."

Zach relaxed as he drove, enjoying the straight road and the silence. Just onto the motorway for the run into the city, Jackie turned, reaching her hand out and stroking his hair. He leaned his head back, dropping his eyelids so he could keep his eyes on the road.

"You're so uncomplicated."

"You really think so? With my mad relatives and my search for who knows what?"

"But you're clear. When I look at you, that's what I see: clarity, and honesty and love. Can I talk to you about something else? Something that's been confusing me."

"Sure."

"It's off the map, really, outside my focus, but it keeps grabbing me and pulling me back."

Zach glanced over, then looked back at the road again. "Sounds serious."

"Not serious, just confusing, like I said."

"So ... what . . ?"

"I've been getting these emails, from another inventor. And there's something ... off. It's a woman, and she talks about how refreshing it is to meet another female inventor."

"You've met?"

"No. But she talks as if she knows me, and knows me well. Anyway, she wants advice, about how to make her invention successful. And I don't know what to say."

"What is it, her invention?"

"I'm not sure, exactly. She talked about it being the next essential kitchen implement. She wants to meet me."

"And . . ?"

"And I don't know. I'm not pulled to it. But I want to help, if I can. I've been lucky, and if there's anything I can do, I'd be glad to do it."

"But you're not sure."

"I wasn't. But saying it out loud makes it clear. I should meet her. Find out what she needs."

"She's local? A New Zealander?"

"Yeah, she lives down south, but she said she'd come up any time I would see her." Jackie nodded, trying to convince herself. "I'll send her an email, set up a time."

"You're still not sure."

"I should meet her. What harm can it do?"

They parked on the road outside Bob's house and walked up the drive. He wasn't home yet. Sandra came to the door to meet them, a huge smile on her face. "The traveller and saviour returns!" She ran down the steps and threw her arms around Jackie. "You have no idea how great life has been. Thank you!"

Jackie grinned. "Bob's enjoying the new job then?"

"I had no idea how worried he had been about money, about the business, until the weight came off him. He was always a good man, now he's happy."

"I'm so glad!"

"Come in, have a drink. He'll be home by six. He'll want to see you."

The boys were playing a video game in the living room. Zach's eyes turned towards the sound of the Formula One simulation. "You go through, Babe. I want to talk to Sandra."

Clara was sitting on the floor playing with a mixing bowl and wooden spoon. Jackie picked her up, bowl and all, and sat her on her knee. "What you got in there?" The bowl was full of small metal cars, clanking around as she stirred them.

"She loves the boys' toys, but she has an unconventional approach to playing with them. They don't approve."

Jackie hugged Clara. "You do what you like, Honey. Live life your way." Clara tapped the device on Jackie's arm and pointed into the bowl. Jackie obligingly took it off and dropped it in.

"She'll damage it!" Sandra protested as Clara stirred it into the mix.

Jackie shrugged. "I can make another one. She knows what she wants, she should have it. It's a rare thing. So tell me about Bob."

"Like I said, a weight has been lifted. And he loves driving that car! He always said the Toyota was fine, but he's like a kid. Keeps offering to go out to the supermarket, pick up any little thing I say I need. I swear he'd go for one item at a time and then go back again."

He drove in at 5:30 and Jackie could see what Sandra meant. He bounded up the steps, whistling, the keys spinning in his hand. He stopped short when he saw Jackie, then lifted her off her chair, spinning her, too. "You're back! It's so good to see you."

Clara, who had toddled out of the room some time earlier, reappeared at the doorway at the sound of his voice. He let Jackie go and picked her up, burying his head in her hair, the image of domestic bliss. Jackie smiled.

Dinner was a warm, happy affair and when Jackie and Zach stood to go, Bob got up to see them out. They walked into the driveway and Bob held out the keys to the Porsche. "Thanks, Sis. It's been fun." His face was a picture of ineptly disguised tragedy.

Jackie looked from him to the car and back again. She put her hand on the bonnet. "That's okay, Bob. You keep it. I don't need it."

His mouth gaped open. "But ..."

"I don't need it, really. It was just a whim. You enjoy it. And I'll borrow it from time to time."

"But ..." The surprise on his face was transforming into the beginnings of an irrepressible smile.

"See? That, that look. That's worth more to me than any sports car." She turned to Zach, whose face was blank with disbelief. "Come on, Babe. Take me home."

53

Jackie met Betsy at a café near the factory, instinct having told her to keep her away from anywhere more personal just yet. She came in gushing.

"I can't believe you'd meet me! I've been dreaming of this for such a long time. Oh my God! You're so young!"

Jackie had held out her hand but took a step back as the woman came up too close, too fast. She was mid-thirties, blowsy hair too large around her face. She had made an attempt at makeup, but the bright red lipstick was crooked and the blusher overdone. 'Blending, that's the key.' The words ran through Jackie's head, she didn't know where she'd heard them. She turned toward the counter to recover from her disorientation. "What can I get you?"

"Cup of tea, please, and one of those muffins. I should pay, really, since you've been so kind as to meet me, but you can afford it, can't you? I'm just starting out, a poor, starving, inventor." She laughed again.

Jackie ordered and paid, then went back to where she had been sitting on a sofa flicking through a magazine. Betsy sat on the same sofa and slid to an intimate distance. "I want to hear all about you! My invention's so much further from finished than yours. And people haven't been very encouraging. That's why I was so glad to have the chance to meet you.

People pull you down, don't they? Especially successful people. That's why I don't join groups, you know. Groups of inventors."

"Are there groups of inventors?"

"They ... well, they're all so self-absorbed, full of themselves, the ones who've made it. And I'm not interested in that. I'm not interested in being told I won't make it. That my invention needs improvement. What about encouragement? What about people actually putting their money where their mouth is and investing? That's what I need." She eyed Jackie hungrily. "Have you made a lot of money, would you say?"

Jackie looked up gratefully as Betsy's tea and muffin were delivered. Her own coffee had gone cold on the table.

"Tell me exactly what it is you've invented."

Betsy puffed out her chest. "It's an orange peeler."

"Like a potato peeler?" Jackie held out her hands, miming the potato-peeling action.

"No! It's a machine, that peels ten oranges at once. And it's scalable. Based on the commercial potato peeler, using friction between the individual fruit."

"And your market?"

"Is huge. Every household in the country, in the world!"

Jackie's eyebrows pulled together as she tried to understand. "Do you think many households will need to peel ten oranges at once?"

Betsy leaned in closer and tapped Jackie on the hand. "Now I won't have any nay-saying." She laughed.

"But I actually quite like peeling an orange, if I'm going to eat an orange. It helps me get into the mood of eating it."

"I'm at the stage of needing help with investment and marketing." Betsy sighed and shook her head. "I had a meeting with a local businessman where I live. I came out quite despondent. But then I realised he was just jealous. His business is dull, boring. No spark. I went to some network groups, but everyone's just out for themselves. I felt as if my head had been talked off with hearing about everyone else's business. And then I saw you, on television. 'That's me!' I thought. 'Give me five years and a bit of support, and I'll leave her standing in the dust.' I'm so glad you agreed to help me. It will be so good to have a mentor, a business partner like you. Someone who has done it, who can lead the way."

Jackie cleared her throat. "Do you have any idea on pricing? What sort of range?"

Betsy shrugged sideways and burped slightly. "At this stage it's uncertain. Around the $400 mark, possibly. I think bread makers started around there. Of course, the price will come down with mass production, and competition."

"But surely competition, the cheaper prices, come from other companies, that wouldn't be ..."

Another admonishing tap on the hand, another laugh. "Nay-saying again!"

Jackie took another tack. "What about the jam factories? Marmalade. That might be a potential ..."

"Too difficult. Those big companies, impossible to get into."

"Well, do you know how many there are, world-wide?"

"No. Not interested."

Jackie picked up her wallet and phone. She had arranged for Zach to meet her in a couple of minutes, to come in if she wasn't finished. She hoped he was on time. She stood. "Well, Betsy, it was a pleasure to meet you. I wish you luck."

"You're not going! I had so many more questions."

"I have another appointment." She turned, tangling up with Betsy as she tried to finish her tea, wrap her half-eaten muffin and stop Jackie, all at once.

"Just another couple of questions?" She stood in front of Jackie, blocking her exit. Jackie glanced out into the car park. No sign of Zach yet.

"All right." She sat down.

"It's about development. At the moment the fruit keeps bruising, splitting. I'm getting pulp more than nicely peeled oranges. Can you tell me, how do I get it to work?"

"Ay up! There's my ride." Jackie stood more quickly this time and jumped over Betsy's legs before she had a chance to stand. She held out her hand momentarily, then pulled it back, wiping it on her jeans. "It really has been an experience meeting you. All the best."

She reached the car at a run and was in the passenger seat before Zach had turned off the engine. "Drive!" she ordered, and as they left the car park she began to laugh.

"Well?"

Jackie quelled the laugh and shifted in her seat, as always calmed by Zach's presence. She pursed her lips and let out a controlled breath. "I get a lot of emails, a lot of requests for help. Usually they're things I can answer quickly, or refer on to someone else. Why did I want to meet this one?"

"Tell me. What happened?"

"I can sum it up in one word. Deluded. She said she wanted to hear all about me, but all we talked about was her, and the people who haven't been supportive. Chalk me up on that list, I'd say. Goodness knows what she'll say about me now. 'All she could do was talk to me about marmalade factories! Marmalade factories, I ask you!'" The accuracy of her imitation after such a short meeting disturbed her, and she shook her head and her arms to clear herself. "I want to get that one out of my psyche. Crazy!"

Zach smiled.

"What? What's funny?"

"I'm trying to remember where I heard it, who said it."

"Said what?"

" 'You know you're successful when you start attracting nutters.' "

"Well then, here's to success! Nice to know I'm successful, but do the nutters need to keep coming?"

"I think that's up to you. Where now?"

"Mike," said Jackie, in a small voice. "Next we're meeting Mike."

"Exhibit B." said Zach, drily.

"You're not jealous any more?"

"Jealous? I was never jealous!"

"Oh, right."

"So then, where are we meeting nutter number two?"

"Mason's office. He said he's got some ideas for the Mood Meter. Groundbreaking, he said. So let's go."

54

Mason let them in showing signs of impatience. "Do I need to be here? I've got things to do."

Mike looked at him nervously, but stood his ground. "Yes. What I've got to say is important."

Mason pulled out a chair from the board table and sat down. The others followed. "Well?"

Jackie leaned forward towards him. "Good to see you, Mike. You look well. Happy."

Mike held up his arm. "It's this. I never realised how much time I spent upset. Even when I thought I was fine. I'd tell a joke, thinking I just meant to be funny, but this would tell me I was agitated. So I started looking at my life, thinking about it. Then I just decided. I'd heard about this retreat, in India, meditation. I took an advance on my credit card and I went."

"We know this much already," said Mason. "We know you went to India. What else?"

Jackie looked at Mason. "But we didn't know about the mood stuff." She turned back to Mike. "You were saying, the humour was to cover up ..."

"Insecurity. But you knew that, right?"

Jackie tilted her head back and forth. "It wasn't my place to tell you. You had to work it out in your own time."

"But you did tell me."

"I don't think ..."

He held up his wrist again. "With this."

"Okay," Mason interrupted again. "India."

"So I went to this ashram, and it was all meditation. It took me a while to get into it, to start, and then the device started beeping when I was about five minutes in. Once I got to alpha state. They didn't like it, so I had to turn it onto vibrate only – great feature, by the way. The person next to me would hear, but not the swami guys. But then the weird thing was, once that started happening, I got faster and faster. After a few days I could switch in, in a second. Watch." He closed his eyes, and a moment later opened them again, embarrassed. "Guess it doesn't work all the time. Mason, can you stop staring at me. I'll try again." And a second later a look of peace came over his face and the Mood Meter beeped.

Jackie sat back. "Wow!"

"I know! Instant meditation."

Mason and Zach looked at each other. "So?"

Jackie hissed. "Don't you get it? This sort of personal mind control, it's fantastic! There's so much scope for – God! – evolution! This could be the next step of evolution."

"No delusions of grandeur or anything."

"Look at him!" She threw her arm towards Mike. "What was he? Uptight, arrogant, a pain." Mike's face fell and his eyes widened. "Sorry. But now he's peaceful, confident, inspirational." Now his chest puffed up. "And not influenced by the opinions of others." She threw him a look out of the corner of her eye and they both laughed. Again, Mason and Zach stared at each other. "Do you really not get it?" They shook their heads. "Well, you will." She turned back to Mike. "What else?"

"How did you know there was more?"

"What else!"

"Well, the alpha state is just the start of meditation. Deeper is the theta state, and then maybe more."

"You don't mean . . ?"

"Yeah. You know that feature, where you can hit the button twice to reset the alert position? I managed to register the theta state and reset it for there. And now I can do that, too."

Again, Jackie sat back. An awed silence descended. Mason broke it with a cough.

"I can show you, but only if the sceptics leave."

Jackie turned to Mason. "Can you behave?"

"No. This is too much mumbo-jumbo for me."

"Zach?"

"Okay. I'll shut up and stay still over here."

"Okay, Mason, go. Do what you have to do. Are you seeing Pandora?"

"This afternoon."

"Well, ask her what this means. Tell her Mike can generate alpha state in five seconds, and theta in ... how long?"

"About ten," Mike answered.

"Have you got that? Will you tell her?"

"All right. Okay."

"And maybe when you see her reaction, you'll be impressed."

The door closed behind Mason. "Okay. Ready."

Mike wiped the smirk off his face and composed a serious expression.

"Do you need to do that look beforehand?"

"No, I just thought it would impress you."

"Well, go on. Let's hear those beeps." And just a few seconds later, the beeps came. Jackie put her hands on the table, blew a breath out and closed her eyes. "I can feel it. Can you feel it?" Her eyes opened again, and she turned to Zach, whose own eyes were wide and staring.

"What was that?"

"You were just in the presence of theta state. It doesn't happen very often. It's amazing."

"Only thing is, I get so excited, I come out of it again."

"Well, meditation was never supposed to be a competitive sport. If you do it to impress, you'll lose it. But you've had times when you've stayed in it?"

"Yeah, wow, amazing. But only when I'm on my own."

"Well, congratulations. Enjoy it. And thanks."

"For what?"

Jackie held up her Mood Meter. "You've opened up a whole new world, for me, and for this." She walked around the table and kissed him. Zach stood up, knocking over his chair. "Not jealous, huh?" Jackie said, without turning.

Zach didn't answer.

"I'm sorry. I just had to check." She turned her head to face him with a sparkle of mischief in her eyes.

55

"What are you doing?" Zach leaned over Jackie's shoulder to see her computer screen.

"I'm organising a meditation retreat."

"Why? Is it that Mike creep?"

"Oh, get over it. He's got a girlfriend now, did you know?"

Zach's face brightened. "Really? Who?"

"Someone he met at yoga. He said it's a great place to meet chicks."

"I'll have to try it," Zach grumbled.

"I'm sorry, I know I've been preoccupied. Just, I'm so excited about this. Come here." She pulled him around to the side of her chair and swivelled around to meet him, pulling his face down to give him a long, passionate kiss.

"You see, you do that," he said, once he had recovered, "and then you're gone again."

Her eyes were back on the computer screen. "I just need to send out this email. We'll make a date for tonight, okay?"

His eyes lightened and he nodded. "Okay. Shall I go buy some champagne?"

"Yeah, good idea." But he knew he had lost her, back in her world of plans and dreams.

The retreat filled quickly, and Sheila, the instructor, was fully engaged in the idea. "It will put me out of a job, though," she joked.

"No. It will make it accessible. So many people don't meditate because they think they won't be able to do it. This will make it easy."

"If you say so."

Mike was employed as consultant advisor, to observe and add refinements when he saw they would make a difference. His girlfriend was coming, and Carlotta and Craig. "You'll have to leave Anna and Victoria in their cages, though, we can't have any distractions."

"Cages! We don't have cages!"

"Well, in your hut then. Promise."

Craig frowned and said nothing. Jackie let it go.

The new blocks were finished and the capacity of the campground was up to 600. Craig had finally decided to let go of the original caravan and empty tent sites and the whole place was a city of Life Tents, each rented by the day or the week or leased for the season. Some of the original ones had been bought outright, but Craig said he wasn't doing that any more. "Leasing gives me long-term passive income. Those that wants to buy them will have to take them away."

"Fine, whatever," Jackie answered. She knew from experience that it was far easier to let Craig have his way.

Pandora was attending, too. "I've never had much time for meditation, but I want to see this theta thing in action." Mason was there because Pandora was, and because Jackie had insisted.

"This is the new thing, the breakthrough. This will make the Life-in-a-Box look like a little pan fire. Come on, Mason, open your eyes."

"It's mumbo jumbo. Can't people be happy just because they're happy? I was born the way I am, sometimes happy, sometimes not. That's just the way it is. I can't help it, and there's no point trying."

Jackie stopped dead. "Is that what this is all about?"

Mason stared at her, like a deer in headlights. "What?"

"You don't want to take responsibility for your life?"

"I don't know what the fuck you're talking about."

"Life just happens, is that what you think?"

"Of course not. I've built my business, my wealth. And yours." He threw out this last point like a gauntlet, to try to throw her off the scent.

"But life isn't business."

"Says she, the inventor, 'if I don't do this, I'm not me.' " He put on a squeaky mimicking voice, insulting.

"But for me it's not about business, it's not about money. That's just a vehicle for changing lives, for getting it out there. I'm asking again. Do you think life, your experience of life just happens? That you're at the mercy of your emotions?"

"Yes. So?"

"Well, that explains why you stopped using the Mood Meter. But what would you get out of believing that?" Her voice was wistful, curious, as if she wasn't asking him, she was trying to work it out herself; like it was an observed natural phenomenon, not an idea out of a conscious being's mouth.

Sheila walked up to them. "Hey there. Are we ready to start?"

Jackie turned in response and entered the larger tent they had constructed as a village meeting house. The others followed in silence.

The tent was empty apart from cushions scattered on the floor. Wide window flaps were open, allowing a solid, continuous breeze to flow. Once they were seated it skimmed the tops of their heads on its journey through and out of the space.

The campground had been cleared of those not participating and once the participants stopped talking, all was quiet. One car hummed past in the distance. Birds sang and a sheep bleated. Virtual silence.

Sheila took a deep breath in through her nose and out through her mouth. Without speaking, the rest followed. Another breath, then another. She closed her eyes. There was a soft clicking sound and Jackie turned to see Craig, watching her, defiant, with Anna on his shoulder. Carlotta sat with Victoria on a seat nearby. Craig pouted, then relaxed as Jackie smiled at him. She put a finger to her lips, and he raised his eyebrows and nodded.

Sheila lifted her left arm, her sleeve falling back to show her Mood Meter. She took another breath through her nose and put her right hand on the Mood Meter, a look of love and serenity on her face. Most of the group followed suit, lifting both arms and placing right hand on left, device-clad wrist. Sheila brought her hands down into her lap, breathed again, then gave a little start as the beeping began. Gently, she pressed the small button on the side. From around the tent, beeps came sporadically, each time creating a small wave of response, and each time, Sheila put her hand on her wrist and breathed peace again.

Then a different beep came, deeper and softer. Jackie knew without turning that it was Mike. The word 'Bastard' floated through her mind and she smiled at this competitive side of herself and let it go. A moment later she achieved alpha state, turned off the beeps and disappeared from awareness of what was going on around her. She entered a floating state, warm and luxurious, where all her dreams came true.

It was a while later – maybe fifteen minutes during which the mood had been punctuated by two or three more theta beeps, each of which set Jackie into competitive beta state so that she had to concentrate again to drop back into alpha – when the sound of a car interrupted everyone. There was a spray of gravel against the tent, the sound of a car door slamming, and a mid-thirties woman with blowsy hair exploded into the scene.

"Sorry I'm late, sorry I'm late, has it started? Ooh! I'm interrupting! Naughty me!"

"Betsy!" Jackie got to her feet and Sheila breathed one more time and gave a gentle clap, bringing the session to a close. "Betsy!" The words escaped Jackie before she could think them through. "Who invited you?"

56

Pandora and Jackie stood aside discussing the results of the session. Mason sat off at a distance, sulking, occasionally glancing over at them with a wistful, longing expression.

"It's promising, really promising. We'll observe some more over the next few days, then work out how to do a proper trial."

"Perfect." Jackie nodded towards Mason. "You tried it then, the sexy thing. How's it going?"

Pandora smirked. "It seems to be working. But I wouldn't say it's making him happy. In bed he's way more passionate ..."

"Too much information!"

"And in between he's grumpy as fuck. Look at him!"

Jackie's eyes met Mason's this time as she glanced over. She looked quickly away, and greeted Mike as he came eagerly towards them.

"What do you think?" he asked, excitedly. "See what I meant?" The two women nodded. They talked through the events, the pattern of alpha beeps they had observed around the group. Their heads were close, deep in conversation, when Mason muscled in.

"What is this? More planning? More scheming? More leaving me out?"

Jackie stood back, stunned. "We're not leaving you out, Mason. You're part of this, whether you like it or not."

"Well, I don't like it! I don't get it! Give me something I can understand. The Life Kits I can work with, but this! It just puts me on edge."

"But why?" Jackie put her hand to her chest, to hold in her frustration. "This is it! This is the thing that will change lives."

"I don't want my life changed. I want to keep doing what I'm doing, get married, have children, settle down. Life was good already."

Pandora took a step back, staring at him. "Does that mean me?"

But before Mason could answer, Mike started laughing. "I get it!" He turned to Jackie. "Don't you get it? He's scared. Scared this will tumble his perfect façade. Mr Perfect, handsome, successful, in control. He can't handle the introspection. He's worried what he might find."

Mason looked like he might hit Mike. "Little upstart."

"Thanks, God-dad." Mike nodded. "Encouraging, as always."

Pandora moved to restrain Mason, turning him towards her. "Did you mean me?"

Mason pulled against her grip.

"See?" said Mike. "I hit it! All these years I've felt inferior, and it's really him. Look at that insecurity!"

"Can it, Turd." Mason's arm pulled back, his hand in a fist. At that moment there was a crash twenty feet away and they all turned. It wasn't easy to see what was happening, but then the shrieks started. Carlotta had flown at Betsy and they were both on the ground.

It was Zach who acted first out of the frozen crowd. “Leave her alone. Get off her.” But it was Carlotta who was on top of Betsy, and she who needed to be retrieved first. “What the hell do you think you’re doing? That’s my gran!” Zach pulled Betsy to her feet and beyond, lifting her into the air and dropping her at some distance, causing her to stumble as she hit the ground. Her face was twisted into grotesque defiance.

“I only said she was wrong. You can’t breathe into the dead just with stories. It’s nonsense. They’re gone. That’s it.”

“Stupid slutting cunt! She’s my gran! Fuck off back where you came from!” Zach turned to Carlotta, who was rocking in Craig’s arms.

Betsy’s hair was full of grit and twigs. She looked crazier than ever. “If she can’t take the truth ...”

Jackie walked up to Betsy and slapped her. “The truth. Let’s have some truth. The truth is you’re a self-serving, self-satisfied idiot who doesn’t have a clue about the world and doesn’t give a fuck about anyone in it. It’s all about you. Who gives a toss about peeling oranges? How is that going to help the world, make it a better place? Answer me!”

“I ...”

“What gives you the right to put a hole in other people’s dreams? And how do you know what makes people live? What do you even know about yourself? Your only responsibility is to know yourself. Have you done that?”

Jackie turned to the group. “All of you! Have you done that? That’s what I wanted to do with this.” She held up her wrist. “I wanted to help everyone to know themselves, to live their truth. Carlotta, Craig, Pandora, you’ve got it. Mike, you’re on your way, if you’d stop being a bastard for long enough to let it stick. Mason, God, you’re great! You’re so talented.

But open your eyes, look at yourself. You're a coward when it comes to looking at yourself, you're holding yourself back, and in the process you're trying to hold me back, too. And Zach ..." she held out her hand, sobbing. "Why won't you trust me? I love you, I just want to rest in your arms. Why won't you let me?"

Zach's eyes opened wide. He took his hand from Carlotta's shoulder and reached it out towards Jackie, then let it fall. His face was stricken. Jackie turned and walked away, down the hill, towards the gate and through it. She kept walking. They could sort things out for themselves. She was done.

57

It was Mike who caught up to her a couple of kilometres along the road, opened the passenger door to his car and told her to get in. She did so, sulkily, staring straight ahead as he sat there, engine idling. "What?" she grunted. He looked at her for a moment longer, then straightened up and started driving. "So you're the delegation," Jackie said, finally. "What did they tell you to say?"

"That they're sorry, Mason especially. He said he knows he's put you under pressure, and it's not fair."

"So why didn't he come?"

"He's embarrassed. He thought you'd be angry. And also, he and Pandora are celebrating their engagement."

Jackie looked up, smiling despite herself.

"And Zach. He said he's sorry. He gets it. He's sorry he didn't believe you before."

"And he let you come after me?"

"I told him to get a grip, that you've never been interested in me."

"Am I supposed to apologise for that?"

"No, I am, for being an ass."

"And Carlotta? Is she okay?"

"She's fine. She said she shouldn't have let the little upstart get to her. She's got her pride back."

"And physically?"

"She's stronger than me."

"What about Betsy? I've never been so nasty to anyone before, ever."

"She's sitting on a log, thinking. Crying. But actually, I think she'll be fine. If she's anything like me, she probably needed to hear the truth, and no-one's had the courage or interest to tell her before."

"I feel bad about it. It's not like me to go off like that."

"You were honest."

"I'm usually more measured, calmer."

"Yeah, I know. That's your miracle. But it had to break sometime. You had to lose your cool."

"You say it like it's a good thing."

"It's not bad. We were never supposed to be perfect."

"Perfect!" Jackie snorted. "I'm a long way from perfect."

"That's just it, Sweetheart ... Okay, sorry, Jackie ... you're too close to perfect for your own good."

She stared out the window again, trying to get her head around this. She gave a little shake. "I just follow my heart. I just do what my heart tells me to do."

"Like I said, that's your miracle. And finally, it's starting to rub off on the rest of us. Thanks."

They had come around in a circle. Mike turned back into the campground driveway and slowed down to crunch through the gravel. They wound up towards the big tent, watched by the crowd. Jackie hunched down in her seat. "Do we have to?"

"Come on."

Zach opened her door and lifted her out into the air. She felt hands on her back, on her shoulder, the flutter of wings against her cheek.

Zach put her down and kissed her on the forehead. He jerked his head to where Mason and Pandora were standing arm in arm. "They've set a trend. What about you and me?"

Jackie nodded, her eyes creased with emotion, half laughter, half tears. She walked over to Carlotta, crouching down near where she was sitting. "You okay, old lady?"

"I'm fine, don't you worry about me."

"And those spirits, are they safe in their stories?"

"I should have known, they were safe all along. She just got to me, with her needling talk. I spit on her."

"You do that. Shall I ask her over nearer so it's more convenient?"

The old woman cackled. Betsy looked up towards the noise, nervous. Jackie walked over to her, stood in front of her and waited. Betsy looked up into her face and pulled herself slowly upright. "Do you think I can? Do something useful? Something that will help people?"

"You can do whatever you want to do."

"I wish I could learn from you."

"Maybe at a distance. Send me an email."

Sheila stepped up to them. "Are we going to continue? We had another meditation session scheduled for about now."

"Sure," Jackie responded. "But I think I'll make my apologies. I need some time on my own. I just need a few minutes with Mason, and then I'll get out of the way so you can start." She jerked her head towards Zach, calling him over. They walked towards where Mason and Pandora stood. "So," she said, looking into Mason's eyes. "What next? Are we still partners?"

"Think so." He was grinning.

"How can you look like that, after all this drama?"

"I like drama. Hadn't you figured that out? And I got what I wanted."

"So do I get what I want? To market the Mood Meter, and change the world?"

"Yeah, if you like."

"And you'll follow up with the Life Kits, make us our fortune?"

"Sure. Mike will help."

"You speaking to him again, then?"

"Sure, why not? Fight's over."

"Boys!"

"You say that, as if there's something wrong with us, but you're just the same."

Jackie laughed and looked at Pandora. "Keep him in line, will you? I'll be gone for a while, don't want him running amok."

Pandora smiled and stretched. "I think I can do that. Threaten to withhold favours. That always works."

"Again, too much information. I'm going. I'll text and let you know where I am." She pulled at Zach's arm. "Come on. Let's go."

58

They got into Zach's car and he started the engine. "Where to?"

"Let's go see Bob, ask if we can borrow his car. I think a road trip is in order, over the hills and far away. Time for contemplation."

"In the Porsche?"

"Yeah."

"Cool."

They drove south, down the coast through the South Canterbury towns: Ashburton, Timaru, then into Otago, through Oamaru, Dunedin, and inland to Cromwell, Alexandra and Queenstown. They stopped on the side of Lake Te Anau, looking out over the water.

"See the way the reflection works, smooth here, where the lake edge blocks the wind, and further out, just the small breeze breaks up the reflection, gives it opacity."

Zach didn't answer. He knew she was just thinking aloud.

"The thing that amazes me, is how the sun trail always leads right to my feet. Wherever I stand, the path leads to me, so that wherever I happen to be, I can step onto it and work my way back to the source, find my way home."

"Most people would say the path starts where they are, and leads into the distance."

"No. The goal is the starting point. I work backwards from there."

"If only I'd known that, it would have saved me a lot of confusion."

"But don't you see, how easy it makes things? If you start with the certainty of the goal, life is so much simpler."

He took a breath through his nose. "I can't keep up with you."

"Don't think about that! Just try to see what I'm saying."

"It's like that moment when you incited me to fall off the world."

"Sort of. But this is easier. Try it."

"Start with the goal in mind, and ... what was it?"

"Create certainty."

"How do you do that?"

Jackie's face flexed through a frown. "Well ..." She squinted off into the distance. "Like when I'm inventing something. There's always a way to do it, but you have to be really clear what it is you want to do. Like the Life-in-a-Box. First I thought about the life I wanted. Bob was getting married, and I didn't want to be in the way. They said it was fine for me to stay, but I wanted them to have a fresh start, just the two of them. So I thought, how would I want to live, if I were living alone? I thought of buying myself a house, but even if I'd been able to afford it, it felt cold, no life to it. Mum and Dad had taken us on camping holidays, and that was fun. Simple, primitive. Those were the best times of my life, when they were there, with nothing to do that I couldn't help with. Just cooking, washing up, washing clothes. Then the fun stuff, walking on the beach, playing tennis. I loved it, every moment full and pure and without anything waiting to be done. So I built my life around that. And I wanted it easy and complete and efficient. So I started with the tent, the bed, the table and chair, and went from there."

"So you knew what you needed, and then you built it."

"Exactly."

"And then?"

"And then I needed money. I was working in a supermarket to pay my way, but that got ..."

"Boring? Mind-numbing? Insufferable?"

"It didn't allow me to be fully me. So then I started at the market – you remember."

"No. I came later, remember, just a couple of years ago."

"Wow, yeah. It feels like you were there forever, but then I remember when you came, it was like ..." She put her hand to her chest and gave it a little flutter. Zach laughed. "So then I realised, I had a way of living, a lifestyle, that was totally free, but I wasn't really happy. I'd have these moments: days, weeks, sometimes a month or more, when everything would go black, for no apparent reason. So I thought, it would be great if I could see that coming, and I imagined a small thing on my wrist that would let me know. I'd read about cognitive therapy, thought replacement, and it worked sometimes, when I remembered to do it, but more often I was down the slope too far before I realised. So that's where the Mood Meter came. Hey!"

"What?"

"I just realised. I haven't had that, the blackness, for ..." She tried to count back. "I can't remember when the last time was. It was at the beachfront campground. So that's at least ... a year ago?"

"So now you've done that. What next?"

Jackie smiled, a slow, deep smile. "That's what we're here to find out. Let's drive."

They drove through to Milford and took the last two places on an overnight cruise on Milford Sound, a group of relaxed, happy people with nowhere to go and nothing to do for 16 hours, milling around, making quiet conversation, eating dinner and when darkness descended, pulling out packs of cards, bottles of wine. Deep, unhurried calm settled over the boat and over the whole Sound.

Jackie woke in the night and propped herself up so she could see out the porthole to watch the stars. Zach snored gently in the other narrow bed. The lift and fall of the gentle waves made it look like the stars were moving.

"What next? What next when I already have everything I need?"

59

As they drove up the spectacular edge of Lake Wanaka next day her heart expanded with the exhilarating beauty. How could she capture this, this rapture, this unbelievable, awe-inspiring experience? Life was good, comfortable, easy, full of love, but this was another level. She wanted to be able to bottle it, to come back to it whenever she wanted. But what was it, really? Light falling on her eyes in a particular way. Nothing but internal experience, brain cells firing, creating emotion, a body experience. How could light falling on her retina cause her chest to expand? What was that part of herself that tried to bear this, to respond to it in a way that did it justice? The lake passed behind them and she wanted to cry, until the grandeur of the Haast Pass took over, clouds trapped in lines and wisps, unable to find their way out of the majestic labyrinth.

"Let's stop here."

"But it's the middle of nowhere."

"We'll find a path."

"It's madness. If we get lost here, we'll be lost forever."

"Just a little way. I'll know how to get back."

Zach wrote a note and left it on the front of the car. "So they'll be able to recover the bodies," he joked.

“Not funny. Relax. Trust me.” She stepped off the gravel verge and down a steep bank, arms stepping from tree to tree as her feet slipped under her. The sound of the river crashed below.

“Jackie!” Zach’s voice was tense. “We’ll never get back up here.”

“Yes. We will. Come on!”

“No. I’m staying here. So I can call Search and Rescue.”

“I want you with me. I always want you with me.”

He laughed, slightly hysterical. “You know that’s not true. Solitude. Contemplation. But be serious. Stay here. Let’s get going. We can take one of the paths later. Walk up to a glacier. Jackie!”

But she had disappeared among the trees. He leaned back against the car and looked at his watch.

Jackie turned and looked up the bank again, taking her bearings, grabbing a landmark so she could navigate back again. She knew she was onto something, that everything was right. The noisy silence of the bush overtook her. Rushing water filled the gaps between notes of birdsong. It had been dry for a few days, and the cliff-side waterfalls were running to a trickle. Get to the river. That was what her instinct told her. It wasn’t dangerous: her instinct was always right.

Ten minutes later she reached the river, roaring as it fell steeply, rushing over smooth boulders, long submerged and sculpted. The flow was fast, white, but peaceful. There was some turbulence as it rolled into gaps between the stones, but mostly there was no resistance, just the action of gravity – fall, land, roll, fall again. Jackie closed her eyes and became the flow of the river. It felt good, natural. This was life: idea, plan, do, market, start again. She had fought with Mason for the right to focus on the Mood Meter, but once it went to market, there wasn't much for her to do. If she wanted, she could delegate the reprogramming to Pandora and bow out completely. There were questions to be answered, ideas to follow up, but it was all easy and automatic now. So what next?

She watched the river and knew the idea was right there, that she just had to trust the process and wait for it. Just like the river would not suddenly decide to stop and die on the next boulder, her next idea and experience would come without her asking. Just wait. Trust. It's easy. She smiled, her eyes closed. She could almost sleep here, she was so in her rushing, roaring element.

A few minutes passed, and suddenly her body froze and she knew something was happening. She opened her eyes and looked across the river, and it was like staring at her own reflection, a miracle. There, standing in the still shallows just under the steep bank, was a tall, long-legged bird. Like an ostrich, or an emu, but different. It stared at her with dark eyes, against a dark, enigmatic face. Its dark, inadequate wings were folded against its sides, almost invisible in the shadows of the overhanging trees. A moa. Believed extinct.

Jackie stood and lifted her hand to shade her eyes. She blinked. No-one would believe this. Like so much else in her life that it was more sensible to keep to herself, she would have to tuck this away in her heart. Well, she would keep it there, this encounter, like a talisman, to remind her that whatever other people thought, she could always trust her instinct.

Five long seconds passed, ten. Then a minute, two, five. Her heart beat in time with the rush of the river. The bird blinked, dipped its head and drank. Jackie lost herself in sympathy with it, unique, lonely, free.

She scrambled up the bank, finding her bearing using the images she had made with her backward glances on the way down. It took a good half hour, slipping back three out of four steps, but finally she came out ten metres from the car. Zach turned towards the scrabbling noise of her final ascent and swore. He walked over and held out his hand, pulling her up without speaking. He opened the door of the car and slammed it after her, getting in himself and driving off without a word. Jackie tried to hold her mood, but felt it slipping. She smiled a rueful smile. She'd have to tell him her story another day.

60

It was two years later. Zach was strapping their son, Anthony, into a front pack so he could give Jackie a break to get some work done. The rigid walls around her were still surprising, even though it had been she who decided she wanted quiet and privacy to bring up her child – for the first little while, at least.

Her two boys walked down the stairs of their apartment, down the gravel drive and along the road to the park. She felt her heartstring stretch to go with them, allowing herself this moment of attachment before she turned back to her latest project: a mobile school.

Why should classrooms be static? Why should learning be theoretical? Now she had a child of her own, her focus homed in on how to bring him up with his natural brilliance nurtured, enhanced, developed. In between breast-feeding and consulting for Mason in their old company, she was studying for her Bachelor's degree in education. So much for not being suited to university: she was loving it, and arguing with the basic premises of everything she learned.

"You can't say that!" she protested. "That's not true for every child." And they listened. They heard her. It was magic.

She was watching young Anthony closely, observing and documenting every alteration and expansion. When he learned to grab his toes, she saw a light go on. 'This is me!' She watched it, fascinated. She read books and looked up journals and found the latest research, and added her private, sometimes dissenting thoughts. For the inventor, there was a miracle here, so much learning and insight, so much transferable information, so much that would lead to new discoveries, new ideas.

In a world of two and a half billion parents, how had no-one seen this before? She dismissed the question. It wasn't helpful. If she was the first, she was the first – it didn't make any difference, and it would not help her use the information, or increase her confidence that she was right. This level of uniqueness was so improbable, she was best not to think about it at all. Just in case, as with Douglas Adams' idea of God, she would disappear in a puff of logic. She was new, she was a miracle, and she had to go on.

She muttered to herself as she worked, feeding herself her working mantra: "Focus on what I want and go for it. And let everything else fall away."

~~~~~~~~~~~~~~~
~~~~~~~~~~~~~~~

If you have enjoyed

Inventor

please post a review on Amazon.

You can also “follow the author” on Amazon
to get notified of new titles as they are published.

Email jennifer@theflowwriter.com
or find out more at theflowwriter.com.

With my very great thanks,

Jennifer.

www.ingramcontent.com/pod-product-compliance
Lightning Source LLC
Chambersburg PA
CBHW061945170626
46813CB00006B/2542
9780473185299